Lady in the Lake

SUNCOAST PARANORMAL 3

by

Lovelyn Bettison

This is a work of fiction. Names and incidents are products of the author's imagination. Any resemblance to actual persons living or dead is entirely coincidental.

Copyright © 2020 Lovelyn Bettison
All rights reserved.

Nebulous Mooch Publishing

2020

Chapter 1

Cheryl leaned forward and put her hands on the dashboard. The world spun around her.

"Are you okay?" Adam asked.

When she decided to come back to Ridge Point, she knew she couldn't do it alone. It was a given that Adam would go with her, despite all the trouble she'd caused. He didn't want her to face her ex-husband, Mark, alone, and frankly, she didn't want to either. "I just feel a bit sick," she said.

The nausea had started long before they rolled up to her old house. The tiny white bungalow was so much smaller than the other homes in town. She and Mark had gotten it for cheap. It was kind of a wreck when they moved in, but she had loved it. They'd put so much care into fixing it up. Now it stood neglected. Weeds overran the once colorful flower bed. Splintered gray wood peered out from beneath flaking white paint.

Adam looked over at her. "You should've stayed back at the hotel. Why don't I take you back now?" He put the car into drive.

Cheryl shook her head as best as she could. The nausea was coming over her in waves. "Give me a minute." She took a few deep breaths and tried to imagine what it would be like when Mark finally paid for his crimes.

She looked over at Adam, who watched her with a worried expression. "We don't even have a plan. I can take you back."

They didn't need a plan. Cheryl thought they would walk up to the front door and knock. In her mind, Mark would be a husk of the man he once was, fragile and sick from too much alcohol and too many cigarettes. He'd answer the door in a pair of torn jeans and a soiled T-shirt. He'd say something like, "What do ya want?" Then Cheryl always pictured herself punching him square in the jaw. He'd fall on the floor in shock. None of that was very realistic, but it was what she fantasized about so often that someplace deep down, she started to believe it could happen.

"I know." She sat up and looked out the passenger-side window. Mark's battered red pickup wasn't even in the cracked-concrete driveway. "He's probably not here anyway."

"Should I knock?" Adam asked.

Cheryl had wanted to be the one who knocked, but even though she was sure he wasn't home, she couldn't bring herself to get out of the car. Her legs were weak under the weight of the past. "Go ahead. I'll watch from here." She stuck her hand in her jacket pocket and felt the small plastic baggie of powder her mentor, Day, had given her before they left. Dragon's blood, devil's dung, stinging nettles, and angelica were all herbs she knew well. Day had given her the powder to protect her during the trip. "You never know what will happen," she'd said.

Adam walked up to the house. He was so calm that it impressed her, but he had no reason to be afraid. He'd never met Mark and didn't know what he was truly capable of. He rang the bell. Cheryl held her breath. A flurry of scenarios ran through her head. In the worst of them, Adam ended up dead. In the best, Mark did.

She hoped she was right and Mark wasn't home. She

hoped they'd go out for a nice lunch and forget about all of this. Maybe they'd drive back to Florida and think of this as a silly misadventure. Then someone opened the door. Cheryl couldn't see who, but Adam didn't talk to whoever it was long. He shook his head as he walked back to the car. It wasn't good news.

When he got in, he brought a puff of cold winter air in with him. "He doesn't live here anymore."

"What?" She had always imagined him still in that house, drinking himself into oblivion while watching ESPN on their blue and white checked couch.

"The woman I talked to said she moved in just a few months ago. It was a foreclosure. She had no idea who lived in the house before her." He started the car.

"I can't believe it. I always assumed he would still be here." She hoped the new occupant would love the house as much as she had, but Mark's absence left a hollow feeling in her chest. Even though she ran away from her marriage and the house, it was a part of her history. Knowing that someone else was living there meant it was time to let go.

"Where to next?" He was already pulling away from the curb.

She had hoped to get a nice lunch, but the change of gears seemed so abrupt. "Give me a minute." She looked out the window as the familiar houses rolled by. She'd driven this road every day for years, and it was still exactly the way she remembered. The houses stood unchanged, as if the march of time didn't matter. She remembered all of the morning walks she used to take and the old lady who lived across the street who used to give her cuttings for her garden. The time she spent in that little house wasn't always bad. They'd had a few good years before Mark turned into a monster. The good times still weren't that great, and the terror she endured overshadowed everything. Her stomach growled.

"Are you hungry?" Adam asked, nodding toward her growling belly. "We should get some food."

"There's a little place I used to like in the center of town."

Adam slowed down as they approached a quiet intersection. "Which way should I go?"

"Pullover," she said. "It's easier if I drive."

**

The tiny diner sat in the center of town, right across the street from the police station. Adam took note of the convenient location. He'd been pushing for them to go straight to the police ever since they got into town. Cheryl wanted to do things differently. Since she was dealing with so many demons from her past, he decided to let her call the shots.

A birdlike waitress with even brown skin and a buzz cut showed them to their table. When he opened the menu, Adam was surprised to be confronted with a list of foods he'd never seen before. He was expecting typical diner fare.

"What is this?" he asked.

Cheryl, whose mood had suddenly brightened, said, "Oh, I should've asked if you like Ethiopian food."

"I don't know. I never had it." He looked around at the restaurant's burnt-orange vinyl booths and Formica tables edged in metal. The only hint that it served Ethiopian cuisine was the flag striped with green, yellow, and red hanging behind the register.

"It's amazing. You'll definitely like it." Her enthusiasm convinced him before the food ever arrived.

They ate from a large round tray using pieces of spongy flatbread to pick up their food instead of silverware. She was

Lady in the Lake

right. It was divine and so full of flavor that he couldn't understand why he hadn't eaten Ethiopian food before. "This is amazing," he said.

Cheryl leaned over the table with greasy fingers, her shirt nearly sagging into a pile of spicy lentils. "I remember the day this place opened. I couldn't believe we would have such an exciting restaurant in this little town, and I was determined to make sure it succeeded. I told everyone I knew, especially the few clients I had at the time. They were packed on opening day, and I knew most of the people. I used to come here all the time and have tried everything on the menu." She tore off a piece of bread and used it to grab a mouthful of chickpeas. "I like to think that I'm single-handedly responsible for their success." Pride shone in her eyes. "I know it's silly, but if it had closed, I would've been heartbroken."

"It looks like they're still doing good." Adam looked around. Even though they were in the restaurant during off-hours, there were customers at many of the tables. "It must be packed in here once dinnertime hits."

"There was always a wait for dinner." She put more food in her mouth and bopped up and down on her chair like an excited child.

She'd oscillated between depression and terror during the trip, so Adam was glad to see her happy. He knew he should savor the moment now because once they found Mark, he wasn't sure what would happen. "How did you meet Mark?"

"We went to college together. He was a philosophy major like me, and we had a few of the same courses. He wasn't a bad guy back then. He was nice and hilarious. He could make me laugh so hard. Looking back, I can pick out a few things that seemed a little off in the beginning. He would get so sensitive about little things and snap at me, but it didn't happen much. I knew he'd had a rough childhood, so I made excuses for him. I wish I hadn't ignored the signs back then. Who knows what my life would be now if I hadn't." She popped the bundle of food into her mouth. She held up her finger as she chewed, something she always did when she wasn't quite done with what she was saying. She swallowed and continued her story. "One time, I walked into my dorm room and he was there going through my things. He had my journal open and was looking in my desk drawer. As soon as he saw me, he jumped. I asked what he was doing, and he got all mad like I had done something wrong. At the time, I blew it off. I thought he was just curious about my life, but I think it was something else." The light in her face slipped away. "After we got married, he started going through my phone and my purse regularly. He was constantly asking me questions about where I was and who I was with. It was like he didn't trust me. Eventually, it got to the point where I couldn't even leave the house without him unless I was going to work." She picked up a napkin and wiped her fingers. "Looking back, I wonder why I let it all happen. I know it's bad to blame yourself, but I just don't understand what I was thinking."

"When you're in the moment, it can be hard to see what's really going on." Adam tore a piece of flatbread that had soaked up the juices of the food from the tray. "When did he start hitting you?"

Cheryl bit her lip and looked down at the table.

"I'm sorry. I shouldn't have asked." Adam wanted to know so badly but also realized that he couldn't force any of this. Cheryl would reveal her past to him when she was most comfortable.

She got a far-off look in her eyes. "No, it's fine. I should talk about it." She took a deep breath. "It didn't start right away. If it had, I would've been more likely to leave. He lost

Lady in the Lake

his job and wasn't having luck finding a new one. Then he started going out and getting drunk. At first, it was a couple of times a week, but that quickly devolved into a nightly affair. He was a wreck, and we were on a downward spiral. One night he came home super late. It was the first time this happened, and I was worried. I called his phone a million times, and he didn't answer. I called his friends, and they had no idea where he was either. I was just sitting up in the living room, waiting and worrying. I was sure something was wrong, and then he came waltzing through the door at four in the morning. I was glad to see him, but so mad because he put me through all that worry. I kind of got in his face about it, asking him where he was and why he didn't answer my calls. He slapped me so hard I fell. He had never done that before, and it caught me completely off guard. I'd never actually been hit before in my life. I never got into a fight in school. My mother never hit me. It was a real shock." She surprised Adam by laughing a bit. "You know the cartoons where somebody gets punched, and stars float around their head. I swear that happened to me."

The story made Adam so angry that he swore he saw stars too. "Why didn't you leave?" He put the piece of bread in his hand back down on the tray and wiped his fingers on the napkin.

"It was the first time it ever happened, and I was in shock, I guess. I couldn't believe it. The next morning, it felt like it had been a bad dream. Then when Mark finally got up, he apologized like crazy. He said he was sorry and that he would never do it again. Since we'd been together for four years at that point, I believed him. I had four years of what I considered a decent relationship before that day. I know now that the relationship was never really good. He was always controlling and manipulative. I was just too naïve to see it."

She looked down at the tray of food. "I'm stuffed. You can finish it up."

Adam swore that when he met Mark in person, he'd beat him into the ground. "So, it kept escalating then?"

She sat back in her seat. "Yeah. I can't believe I didn't see it before it started. Everyone else in my life did. My friends at school warned me about him. They said he seemed weird and way too intense. I thought his intensity was good. He was passionate about things. I wanted that same kind of passion in my life. I wished I could care as intensely as he seemed to about everything. My mom didn't like him either. When I told her that we were getting married, she frowned and told me that I needed to be careful. At the time, I thought she was just rude. Her advice drove me away from her. Even though my mother only lived a couple of towns over, I stopped seeing her." She went silent for a few moments. "That's one of my biggest regrets. She died in a car accident a few months after we got married." Her eyes went glassy. "She was right the whole time, and she never even got to see me leave him. Part of me is glad that she didn't find out that he was abusing me, or maybe she did. Now that I see that there are ghosts all around us all the time, I sometimes wonder if she was around back then. I look for her but haven't seen her yet. She's probably gone to the other side by now. I like to think she saw me leave him and that she knew it was okay for her to move on."

Adam looked down at the food still on the table. There was so much, but he was stuffed. Wiping his hands and face, he said, "I keep waiting for you to see my parents."

"I guess they don't have any reason to worry about you. You've probably always had a solid head on your shoulders." She grinned.

He chuckled. "You mean a big block head on my

shoulders."

"That too." Cheryl laughed. Her laughter didn't last long.

The glass door of the restaurant swung open, and a small, crooked man limped inside. Stains covered his oversized white shirt. His black pants hung so loosely that he had to hold them up with one hand as he walked. A patchy beard sprouted from his grimy face. Even though he appeared homeless, he walked with a proud stride straight through the restaurant and right up to their table. At first, Adam thought he was going to ask for money. He had reached into his pocket to pull out a few stray dollar bills and held them out to the man, but he didn't care about the money. He focused on Cheryl. Putting both hands on their table, he leaned down and whispered in her ear, "Mark told me you'd be coming back. You couldn't resist, could you?"

Just then, a member of staff, a meaty man that was twice his size, whisked in, taking him by the arm and escorting him out the door. The man didn't protest. He walked proudly, arm in arm with the restaurant staff member like they were part of a royal procession. Before stepping outside, he turned and, looking directly at Cheryl, said, "Till we meet again."

Chapter 2

"What was that about? Do you know him?" Adam asked, watching the man through the tinted front window of the diner as he strutted confidently up the street. His drawn face turned upward into the crisp sunlight of the icy day.

Cheryl shook her head. "No." She paused, biting her lip and looking down at the table for a moment before angling her face toward Adam's. "He mentioned Mark."

"What?" Adam looked toward the window, but the man had already disappeared from view.

"I swear he said Mark told him I was coming back." She chewed the flesh on the inside of her cheek. "I don't know. It's so weird. Maybe I'm just tired." Her nervous gaze jumped around the restaurant before returning to Adam's face.

"Let's find out who he is." He took off across the restaurant.

"Wait! What are you doing?" she called, sliding out of the booth and running after him.

The old man hadn't gone far. Adam had already caught up to him by the time Cheryl made it outside. As she approached, she saw someone completely different than the person who had approached them in the restaurant. His confidence had fallen away, revealing a bent old man riddled with fear. Adam had taken hold of his arm, and the man feebly struggled

Lady in the Lake

against him. "Where's Mark?"

"I don't know any Mark. Let me go." The man's frail voice quivered.

"You said that Mark told you something about me." She looked at his weathered face trying to place it. Was he a friend of Mark's? Had she met him before?

"I didn't say anything about a Mark. I don't know anyone named Mark," he stammered.

The fear in his eyes moved her. Maybe she was mistaken. Her head began to ache. "Are you sure you don't know Mark Hampton?" she asked the man.

"No. I've never heard of him." His face twitched.

"Are you lying?" Adam asked.

Noticing someone coming their way, the man began to yell. "Help! Help me!"

Adam let go of his arm.

"Help!" The man continued to wail.

Their waitress came running up the sidewalk. "You didn't pay your bill." She waved a small black plastic folder in her hand.

"I know. I'm sorry," Cheryl said. "We're going to pay in a minute."

The waitress put one hand on her hip and held out the bill in the other.

Cheryl looked down and realized that she'd left her purse inside. "Let's go back inside, and I'll pay that." She took the bill from the waitress and walked toward the restaurant.

The waitress followed her.

"What about this guy?" Adam called to her.

Just before opening the restaurant door, she turned back to him and said, "He already told us he doesn't know Mark. What else can we do?" All eyes were staring at her when she stepped inside the restaurant. Cheryl rushed over and picked

15

up her purse from the booth. "We weren't going to leave without paying." She made sure her voice was loud enough for everyone to hear.

Adam walked over to the table.

"I'm sorry." She dug through her purse, looking for her wallet. "Being here is bringing everything back to me. I'm freaking out a bit, you know?"

"Of course." He put his hand on her arm. "I'll pay for this."

She looked up at him, searching his face for a clue about what he must think. Did he realize she was coming undone? Would he stay with her as she disintegrated into a helpless heap? She knew coming back here would be hard, but she had no idea how hard until they'd arrived. She sighed. "Am I losing my mind?"

She liked the way he looked at her. He could say so much with one look. His gaze softened. "No, you're not. This would be hard for anyone."

Cheryl kept replaying what the man said in her mind. It wasn't exactly what he said that caught her attention but the way he said it. His inflection was too familiar. Was she hearing things?

"Since the police station is right across the street, I thought we could head over there." Adam pulled his card from his wallet and handed it to the waitress, standing next to Cheryl, waiting to be paid.

She marched it over to the register without a word.

"Go over there and do what? We don't really have anything to tell them." The thought of going to the police now seemed like an exercise in self-torture. "I called them already, and they accused me of trying to get revenge on my ex."

"I thought we could ask some questions and maybe find out about unsolved cases."

Lady in the Lake

The waitress came back over with his card. "Have a nice day," she said because she had to, not because she meant it.

"Thanks." Adam smiled at her, as if not noticing the hostility in her voice.

"I think we can just as easily look that up online," Cheryl said.

"Look, we know that he killed someone--" he began.

"We don't really know that. We're guessing." Cheryl needed to make sure he understood that they didn't really have any evidence.

"You saw him drown that woman." He raised his voice, and the other diners turned to look at them again. The waitress glared at them from across the restaurant.

"We should go." Cheryl locked her arm in his and steered him toward the door.

"We should go to the police station." He took the lead as soon as they got outside, pulling her across the street to the massive, brick building with the police crest on its side. She knew it was a bad idea, but she'd go along with it just to prove to him that she was right.

She slowed at the bottom of the steps that led to the double glass doors at the entrance of the station.

"You can wait outside if you want." He stopped at the bottom of the stairs and turned to face her. He brushed her cheek before leaning in to give her a gentle kiss. "I'm not going to make you come inside. Take the keys and sit in the car." He reached into his pocket, but before he could retrieve his keys, Cheryl was walking up the steps.

"I'll go in."

**

Every chair in the police station lobby was occupied, and

a line of people stretched from the counter to the door. "Jeez. There must be a lot of crime in this town," Adam said.

"It's not usually like this," Cheryl said.

"You've been here before?" He had only ever seen the inside of a police station on TV.

"I almost turned him in one day. It was early on. He'd gotten drunk and knocked me around. I came here to file an assault charge against him." She bit her lip and looked at the floor. "I chickened out and left without talking to anyone."

He didn't know what to say.

"If I hadn't, I probably would've stopped him from..." She stopped herself.

"You had no idea what he could do back then." He wanted so badly to be able to reassure her.

"I think that deep down, I knew. That's why I came in the first place." She sighed. "That's why I left."

"Excuse me," a female voice behind them said.

Adam realized that he was standing holding the door halfway open, blocking anyone from entering the building. He turned to see a young woman with a stroller waiting to get in. He held the door open wide for her. She immediately joined the line. He motioned for Cheryl to go inside.

All the commotion reminded Adam more of a hospital emergency room than a police station. People hurried about noisily, talking to one another. Everyone seemed to be on urgent business, except for the receptionist at the front of the line helping everyone. She wore a bored expression on her heart-shaped face. Adam was too far away to hear what she said to people, but she seemed to talk slowly, taking her time with each person in line. He tapped the woman in front of them on the shoulder. "Is it always like this in here?"

The woman shrugged. "Didn't use to be, but since all those murders have been going on, everybody's lining up to

Lady in the Lake

tell what they know, hoping to get the reward."

"Murders?" Cheryl asked.

"You haven't heard? It's been all over the news for weeks. They found five bodies already. It's scary. That kind of thing never happens here." Her baby began to cry. She leaned over and cooed into the stroller. "They think it's a serial killer, like Jeffery Dahmer or something." The baby opened its small pink mouth and let out another loud cry. "Don't you pay attention to the news?"

"We're not from around here," Adam said.

"Is that why you're here? Do you have a tip to give?" Cheryl asked.

The woman angled the stroller a bit so she could tend to her baby while they talked. "No, I got this in the mail." She reached into her diaper bag and pulled out a large envelope. "They're threatening to arrest me for unpaid parking tickets. Can you believe that?" She looked at them like she expected them to say something.

Both of them shrugged.

"These tickets aren't even mine. They belong to my raggedy brother. I keep telling him that he's got to pay these, and he still hasn't done it. Anyway, I'm here to take care of this nonsense before they roll up on me one day and arrest me. I can't get arrested. I have a baby to take care of." She pointed at the baby.

Cheryl nodded. "Your brother should be here."

She sucked her teeth. "You don't have to tell me." She reached into the stroller to pick up the fussing baby and began to bounce him on her hip.

The line inched forward.

The door behind the counter opened, and a short man wearing black plastic rimmed glasses came out. He sat at the chair next to the slow-moving receptionist. "Next," he called out. His deep, booming voice surprised Cheryl.

He was fast-talking and all business, so the line started to move along at a faster clip. Once they'd gotten through the line, people were told to sit in the hard, orange, plastic chairs in the lobby to wait. The chairs filled up quickly. People stood, propping themselves up against walls and leaning in corners. Occasionally, a police officer in their dark uniform would come through the double doors at the front of the lobby and call out someone's name. Most of the time, the person called stood slowly, as if their whole body ached from sitting in those uncomfortable chairs, and lumbered over to the police officer, holding one hand aloft before disappearing into the back with them.

"I don't think we should be waiting here. We don't even know what we're going to say. They're obviously swamped." She crossed her arms and looked around the police station.

"What if Mark is the serial killer? No wonder that ghost has been hanging around. We have to stop him before he kills anyone else." He spoke in a hushed tone, but he saw the woman in front of him turn her ear toward him as he spoke. Her baby had dropped off to sleep in her arms almost as abruptly as it had started crying.

"We don't know for sure that Mark is involved in this. We don't even know if he's still in town."

"But what if he is? What if this is our chance to stop him from hurting people?" He observed her face. Her jaw tightened for a moment. Then she closed her eyes, her lips moving ever so slightly. When she opened her eyes, a tear slid down her cheek.

"I'm scared that he'll know I'm here, and if he did kill all those people, he'd have no problem killing me."

He put his arm around her waist and pulled her into him. "I won't let that happen," he whispered in her ear. The line inched forward again.

She rested her head on his shoulder, and her hair tickled his cheek.

They didn't say much else to each other as they inched forward in the line. Adam watched the baby in front of them, now sleeping peacefully. Before he knew it, they were next.

"I love the feeling of being next," Cheryl said, swaying back and forth as they stood waiting to be called.

"Neeext," the woman behind the counter said, drawing out the vowel to make the word twice as long as it should've been.

"That's us." Cheryl held up her hand as she walked forward. Adam found her sudden enthusiasm amusing.

"Is this about the Ridge Point killer?" The woman didn't even look at them. "There are a lot of people here waiting to talk to the detectives about it, so the wait will probably be a few hours."

"We're not sure. We have information about a murder, but we don't know if it's related," Adam said.

The woman looked up. Her face sagged. The liner around her eyes was smudged. "The wait will be a few hours then."

They told her their names, and she repeated them into the phone before telling them to take a seat.

They found an empty wall to lean on while they waited. A short, scruffy man in his late forties stood next to Adam. "I can't believe they don't have enough seats in here," he said to Adam. The man scowled as he looked around at the crowded lobby. "They should have more detectives working the case, so we don't have to wait like this."

"Yeah." Adam scanned the room, wondering how many people were there to give a tip about the murders.

"You got a tip for them? Mine is airtight. I'm definitely getting that reward money." The man gave Adam a tight-lipped grin like he was trying desperately to keep a secret.

"We're not here about the murders." Adam didn't know if they were or not. They were there about a murder, but he didn't think it was anything that happened recently.

"Good." The man had a satisfied look on his face. "That means we're not competing for a piece of the reward." He folded his arms across his chest and angled his body away, signaling to Adam that he was done chatting.

The lobby hummed with conversations. "I can't believe how crowded it is." He put his hand on Cheryl's shoulder. She was turned away from him, looking at her phone.

"Yeah." Her tone told him that she wasn't interested in talking right now. That was fine. He could entertain himself.

He pulled his phone from his pocket and looked down just as a large drop of water landed on the screen. He looked up, but the ceiling was perfectly white with no signs of wetness. Another drip landed on his forehead. He looked down and wiped the drip away. Another drip struck the top of his head. The cold water rolled down his forehead between his eyes and down to the tip of his nose before hitting the floor. Then he moved to the other side of Cheryl. "They need to get their ceiling fixed. Something keeps dripping on me." Adam reached up to wipe the water away from his forehead.

Cheryl looked up at the white tiles on the drop ceiling. "I don't see anything."

Another large cold drop landed right in the middle of Adam's head. "That. See that." He pointed straight up.

"I don't see anything." She looked at the ceiling again and then reached up to touch the top of his head. "It's not wet. You must be hallucinating."

Adam reached up and immediately felt the wet spot on top of his head. "Here it is." He placed Cheryl's hand on the spot.

"There's nothing there. Stop messing around." Just as she

Lady in the Lake

took her hand away, another drip landed on the top of his head. This time Adam looked up to see a ghost floating above him. She seemed to be in a bubble of water, her brown hair floating around her head like tentacles. The water wrapped around her. Her arms stretched upward.

Adam didn't need an explanation. He knew her. She was the first and only ghost he ever saw. Pointing up, he asked Cheryl, "Do you see that?"

Cheryl's gaze shifted upward. "See what?"

"She's here. She's right here." Every time he saw her, he experienced a strange mixture of fear and glee. As quickly as she had appeared, the bubble she floated in burst, and water tumbled down on him. He yelled and dropped to the ground. Everyone waiting in the room looked at him.

"What are you doing?" Cheryl asked. She looked around at the room, and Adam could tell from the look on her face that she was mortified. "It's okay. There's nothing to see here. He just gets sudden..." She paused, unsure of what to say. "Sudden foot pain. It's really bad. He's been to the doctor about it, and they just don't know what it is. Everything's fine. Nothing to see here."

The people in the lobby had returned to their conversations before she even finished her explanation.

He knew that he looked like he'd fallen to the floor for no reason at all, but he had fallen for a reason. That was clear when he noticed a gold necklace on the floor against the wall with a star-shaped charm on it. He picked it up. A thin film of green slime covered the pendant. He wiped it away, revealing the initials T.G. carved into the back of the star. Handing it to Cheryl, he said, "Our ghost came, and I think she left us this."

She took the necklace from him and flipped the star pendant over in her hand. "T.G." She bit her bottom lip. "It's a clue, but I wish we had more."

Chapter 3

The detective slouched back in his chair and looked across the dented metal table at Cheryl and Adam. Cheryl glanced around the drab beige room, wondering how many criminals had sat in the same chair she sat in. How many were killers? Had Mark ever been in here? A mirror covered half of one wall. She imagined uniformed officers standing behind it sipping hot cups of coffee as they watched them through the glass. She'd never been in a room like this but had seen plenty on television shows. She knew what happened in these kinds of places.

"We didn't do anything. We're here to give a tip." She had to make sure they hadn't confused them with criminals because the detective was looking at them like he thought they might be.

The detective took the pencil from behind his ear and began tapping it on the tabletop. "So you say you've got some information about the Ridge Point killer?"

He didn't say anything disparaging, but Cheryl could tell by the look in his eyes that he didn't believe they had any useful information at all. She knew he was right. "I'm sorry, Detective..." Cheryl hesitated. "What is your name?"

"Haskell." He looked off to the side when he said it as if introducing himself was beneath him.

"Detective Haskell." She said his name as if testing it out. "I see that you're extremely busy here, and I wouldn't want to waste your time." She started to stand, but Adam reached over and put his hand on her shoulder.

"Go on, tell him." Adam looked at her and gave a little motion with his head.

She hadn't realized when she'd agreed to this that she'd have to do all the talking. She swallowed the lump forming in her throat. There is never a good time to tell a police detective that she could see ghosts. "I'm sorry. I think we had a little bit of a misunderstanding. I don't know anything about the Ridge Point killer."

The detective furrowed his brow. "You've been waiting out there for hours, and now you tell me you don't have any information? Everybody in this town has information."

"She's just kidding." Adam cut in.

"There's a killer out there. This isn't a joke." Detective Haskell shifted forward to stand.

"We think we know about a murder victim. I doubt it has anything to do with the Ridge Point Killer though. She was drowned in a lake a couple of years back." Adam looked at Cheryl when he said this as if expecting her to add something.

"You think? What makes you think that?" Detective Haskell sat back in his chair again.

"Does it matter?" Cheryl asked.

Detective Haskell pulled his chin back in a look of disgusted shock. "Of course, it matters. It matters a lot. Who is the victim? How do you know they were murdered? Do you know the killer? Where's the body? If you can't give me any of these answers, I can't help you."

Cheryl and Adam both blinked at him blankly for a few moments.

"And there you go." The detective stood.

Lady in the Lake

"Just because we don't know the answer to any of those questions doesn't mean it didn't happen," Adam said.

"But it does mean that you don't have a legitimate tip. So you came here to waste my time when I could be talking to someone else who can give me reliable information. Meanwhile, a killer is out there, and for all we know, he could be killing someone else right now." His words were calm and measured, but intense anger bubbled just beneath the surface.

"We have something that belonged to the victim." Cheryl pointed at Adam.

He pulled the necklace they'd just found on the police station floor from his pants' pocket and extended his hand to the detective.

"What's this?" he asked, not moving to take it.

"It's a necklace," Cheryl said.

He scowled. "I can see that it's a necklace. Where did you get it? How do you know it belonged to the victim?"

"Well... Ah..." Cheryl stammered. She had been right. Coming here was a bad idea.

Detective Haskell went to the door and opened it. "You can show yourselves out."

Adam returned the necklace to his pocket and pulled out a business card. "Here," he said as he approached the door. "Take this in case you change your mind and want to talk to us."

Detective Haskell looked at the card for a moment. "Paranormal investigators... Priceless." He let out a deep belly laugh. "Hey," he yelled into the station. "Louie, these ghost hunters came to give me a tip about a murder."

"Is that right?" A balding uniformed officer leaned back in his chair. His eyes followed Cheryl and Adam as they walked through the station.

"You're right. This was a bad idea." Adam took Cheryl's

hand in his.

"We're going to have to figure this out on our own." Everyone had stopped working to turn and look at them.

Neither of them spoke as they walked through the lobby and out the front door into the cold. The brisk afternoon air wrapped around them. Cheryl folded her arms over her chest. It had taken such a short time for her to get used to the Florida heat that the winter chill was nearly intolerable.

"Well, that didn't go well." She stomped her feet on the ground, trying to warm up her legs in her slim-cut jeans.

Adam said nothing. He marched across the street to the car.

They got in, and he started the engine. Cheryl tried to turn on the heat, but it blasted them with cold air.

"It has to warm up first." Adam put the car into reverse and backed out of the space.

"Now what?" Cheryl asked.

"I wish I knew."

**

"This was a bad idea. Why did you let me do this?" Cheryl slouched in her seat.

"You were right, and I was wrong. I was hoping we'd tell them what little we know and they'd be like, 'Great! Here's a list of missing people we have on file.' I know that was naive." Saying what he thought was going to happen out loud made him feel even more foolish than he already did.

She chuckled. "Haven't you ever watched a cop show?"

He laughed. "You probably wouldn't believe me if I told you that I grew up watching all the <u>Law and Order</u> franchises."

"Not after today's display."

Lady in the Lake

He was glad they could laugh about their encounter with Detective Haskell, even though there was a lot at stake. "I say we go back to the motel room and regroup."

"How about we go back to the motel so we can get our stuff and go home is more like it." The lightness in her voice had gone.

Taking his eyes off the road for a moment, he looked at her. She was staring back at him with all the humor wiped away from her face.

"We can't do that."

She shifted in her seat. "Yes, we can."

"You don't really want to. That woman lost her life because of your ex-husband, and now she's asking you for help. You can't let her down. She won't let you let her down because you know if you don't do this, she'll haunt both of us forever. The last thing I need in my life is another haunting."

Cheryl laughed unexpectedly. "The last time you were haunted, it almost drove you crazy. You were a wreck. And the state of your apartment... I couldn't believe it the first time I walked in there."

Adam didn't need a reminder. Those were some of the darkest days of his life. "I saw the look on your face the first time you went to my place." He remembered the embarrassment, but he needed help so badly that he was willing to humiliate himself in front of her. "I can't let my life get to that state again."

"Even if this lady, T.G. or whatever her name is, haunts you forever, I don't think you would ever get into that state again. Now you know what you're dealing with, so it's different. I mean, look at me, I see them all the time now, and I'm totally fine."

Adam smirked. "Are you though?"

She struck his shoulder playfully. "Yes, I am. I'm totally normal--" She chuckled. "--for somebody who sees ghosts all the time and works as a paranormal investigator."

"Totally normal," Adam repeated.

**

Cheryl noticed the paper stuck in the motel room door as soon as they parked. She placed her hand on Adam's shoulder and asked, "What do you think that is?"

"I don't know. Let's go find out." He got out of the car and hurried toward the door.

She followed him, a bit more hesitant. He had already pulled the piece of paper from the door and unfolded it when she reached his side.

"That's weird." He turned the paper so she could read it more easily.

Cheryl read the blocky uneven scrawl. "Welcome back." Her heart sinking, she shook her head. "It could be Mark. I don't know. He doesn't write like this, but nobody writes like this. He must know I'm here." Cheryl looked around the motel parking lot. There were only three cars beside theirs: a battered blue sedan with patches of rust on the hood, a dinged up white minivan parked only two spaces away, and a pristine, bright-red Corvette. Cars raced by on the main road only a few yards away. She realized that Mark could be watching her. He could be somewhere right now, ducking behind a parked car or hiding in one of the buildings nearby, watching them through a window. He could even be checked into this very same motel. This was a bad idea. She hadn't thought the trip through clearly. He had tried to kill her once before. He would probably try again if given the chance, and wasn't that what she was doing by being here--giving him the chance? She was turning herself into a target. Now he could finish what he'd started. Fear gripped her so hard she began to panic. She couldn't get any air. It was as if no matter how deeply she tried to inhale, her lungs wouldn't expand. The world spun around her. Everything was out of control.

"Are you okay?" Suddenly Adam's arms were around her, holding her up as her knees buckled. He got the door open and helped her into the motel room.

Cheryl plunked down into the mustard-colored vinyl chair near the door. Gripping the arms, she took a few deep long breaths, but panic continued to overtake her. Adam said something, but she didn't know what. His words jumbled. Her thoughts raced out of control, each one a scenario more terrible than the last. She put her face in her hands and closed her eyes tightly. She had to get a grip.

Leaning forward, so her elbows rested on her knees, she concentrated on slowing her breath. One long inhalation. One long exhalation. She did this again and again until the wave of anxiety passed over her.

Adam's hand rested heavily on her back. "Cheryl, are you seeing this?" His voice trembled.

She removed her hands from her eyes to reveal a scene she never expected.

Chapter 4

When Cheryl first looked up, everything was blurred, like she was looking through a lens smeared with grease. She blinked, and the scene came into focus. She still sat in the mustard vinyl chair with Adam standing next to her, but in the distance, the motel room bled into an outdoor scene. The walls seemed to have melted away, revealing the crooked silhouettes of trees around a small lake. The large white disk of the moon reflected in the surface of the water. A farmhouse sat at the water's edge, leering at them. Cheryl couldn't quite make out what color it was in the darkness, but something about the unusual slope of the roof pricked her memory. A yellow glow came from a single window on the second floor.

Everything was still--the trees, the water, the air. Crickets chirped rhythmically around them. Pinpricks of light flashed amongst the trees. Someone yelled in the distance, and Cheryl looked up at Adam, who watched with her, unblinking.

"What's happening?" he asked.

"I think she's showing us something." Cheryl was only guessing.

There was another bloodcurdling scream. Adam took a few steps forward, looking like he might try to run into the scene to help.

Cheryl reached out and grabbed his arm. "There's nothing you can do. This already happened. Just watch and look for clues. The more we see, the faster we can solve this and get out of here."

The front door of the house swung open, spitting out two bodies. They rolled off the porch into the flower bed.

"Help!" the woman yelled. She punched the man in the chest again and again. "Get me out of here."

He said nothing, not even a grunt.

"Get away from me!" She stood and ran. "Help! Help!" she yelled, but there was no one else around.

The man stood. He dusted off his pants with a measured calm that terrified Cheryl. She couldn't see his face but doubted that he was Mark because Mark was never calm. He looked up at the woman running and yelling. He ran one hand through his hair before taking off after her.

They were both too far away for Cheryl to make out any of their facial features, but she knew from the yellow dress and the long dark hair that the woman was T.G. Was the man Mark? It couldn't be. She squinted at the scene, hoping to see more details, but that didn't help.

The man was fast, much faster than the woman. He caught her by the hair, whipping her backward. She fell, her head striking the ground. It all happened too quickly for Cheryl to cover her eyes. She didn't want to see any of this, but she had to look.

The woman went limp. Grabbing her under the arms, the man dragged her to the water. His back was facing them now. He got closer and closer, and when he reached the water's edge, he turned around. Cheryl tightened her grip on Adam's arm. She gasped.

There was a scribble of dark marks where his face should've been, like looking at a scratched out face in a photograph. Cheryl shuddered.

"Impossible," Adam whispered.

But it was possible because they were looking at it. No matter how his face was hidden, Cheryl knew Mark when she saw him. He moved with a new calmness and ease that she'd never seen before, but she knew from his measured stride and wiry frame that it was him. She knew him better than she'd ever known anyone. Fear welled up inside of her, but she did her best to push it down. She needed to focus. There was no room for panic now.

At the water's edge, beneath the branches of the willow tree, he dropped her in the dirt. Then twisting around, he turned and looked back at the house. Cheryl looked at the house too and could see a silhouette standing in the top window looking out over the scene. Then the man picked the woman up and threw her into the lake. The shock must have made her come to because she flailed up and splashed around. The man hurried in after her. The woman struck him in the face. He reeled back, and the anger inside him exploded as he hit her and held her down. It felt like hours. Then it was done. He waded out of the water, his clothes clinging to his body. Once he reached land, he looked up at the house again. The figure standing in the window walked out of view before he limped up to the house. He walked slowly, taking his time. When he reached the front door, someone opened it for him, and he disappeared inside before the whole image faded from view.

**

Adam realized he'd been holding his breath and exhaled. Would this ever get easier? Would he ever get used to seeing these ghastly scenes? He looked down at Cheryl, who looked as stunned as he felt.

"Are you okay?" he asked.

She nodded. "I'll never get used to this." It was as if she'd read his mind.

"Me neither." He sat down on the edge of the bed and pulled his phone from his pocket to search for missing person reports. "There has to be some record of her somewhere. It can't be hard to find. Everything is online these days, right?" He looked over at Cheryl, who sat as still as a statue.

She sniffled and rubbed her eyes. "She showed us clues. We have to figure them out." She thought for a moment longer. "I think I might've been to that house before, but I'm not sure. It looks familiar, but I can't place it."

"How long ago do you think you saw it?"

"I'm not sure. I don't even know where it is." She bit her lip. "I think it could be on the edge of town somewhere."

"Maybe we just need to drive around a bit to jog your memory." He pulled the keys from his pocket. "We could go now."

She shook her head. "I need a break. We were at the police station for ages. It's getting late. Can't we just order dinner and rest?" Her voice was weary.

Even though Adam was anxious to solve this, he understood. He was tired too, and when he stopped to think a moment, the idea of getting back in the car wasn't very appealing.

"I guess you're right. It'll still be there in the morning. Plus, we'll have the whole day to look."

"Maybe I'll remember where it is tonight." She tried to sound optimistic. "Right now, I just want to shower and get something to eat."

Adam was looking forward to resting too, but the ghost had other ideas.

Chapter 5

Adam didn't sleep well. The pizza they ordered sat like a lump in his stomach. Just when he had finally drifted off, he awoke with a start to ice-cold water dripping from the ceiling onto his head. He sat up and wiped the drops from his face. He considered waking Cheryl, but she looked so peaceful lying there, her hair draped across her face, her legs tangled in the sheets.

He swung his legs over the edge of the bed, and as soon as he stood, he entered a different world. He was back in the woods looking at the lake and the house. There were no lights on at the house. The only sound was the chirping of crickets. A balmy breeze blew across his face. His feet sank in the grass. The earthy smell of decomposing leaves and mud filled the air. He shivered and crossed his arms across his torso. How he wished he had gone to sleep in more than just boxers.

Undeterred by his state of undress, he walked through the trees to the edge of the lake. Looking in, he saw nothing, only the reflection of the moon in the still, dark water. If he hadn't known what had happened here, it would've seemed serene. He reached down and stuck his fingers in the water. It was ice cold. He wondered if she was still in there or if he had traveled to some different time, one before the incident ever happened. "T.G., I don't know your name, but we're going to get justice for you. I promise," he said into the smooth surface of the lake.

He looked at the house. Should he go inside?

He rose to his feet and hurried around the lake, ignoring the jagged edges of rocks beneath his soles. He crossed the meadow, the tall grass tickling his calves, and walked up to the brick walkway that snaked its way to the house's front door. He passed the black mailbox and, realizing it might give him a clue, doubled back to look at it. The white numbers painted on its side read 4444. He opened it hoping to find a letter, but it was empty. From the outside, the house had a cozy, lived-in look that would never betray the evil he suspected went on inside. Matching shrubs flanked the front step. A terracotta flowerpot sat on the porch with a cascade of ivy pouring over the side. He walked right up to the front door and tried the knob. The door glided open, inviting him in.

Adam hesitated. He looked back at the trees and the lake before deciding to step inside. His bare feet settled into the thick carpet in the narrow entryway. Dark wood paneling covered the walls. The smell of rot assaulted his nostrils as soon as he stepped inside. He wondered if he should go any further. He compelled himself to continue forward, leaving the narrow space of the entryway and stepping out into the living room where a horror show of death confronted him.

Dismembered limbs lay strewn about the living room floor. Dark red stains spotted the beige carpet. Adam stayed near the door taking in the gruesome scene of dismemberment with a strange sense of detachment. His eyes scanned the living room, looking for some evidence of Mark when he noticed something on the floor next to the armchair. He approached it slowly. It couldn't be. Reaching down, he pushed the tangle of dark curls away from the face only to see Cheryl's dismembered head.

He gasped and jumped back, falling onto the floor in a thick puddle of blood. His heart fluttered, and anger welled up inside of him.

"Mark! Mark! I know you're in here somewhere." He ran through the living room and into what he thought would be the kitchen, but once he stepped through the doorway, he found himself back in the hotel room.

It was dark all around them. He noticed that his boxers felt damp. He reached down to touch the damp spot, and when he looked at his hand, it was smeared with blood. It had been real. He crossed the room to check on Cheryl, who was still sound asleep. He put his hand on her shoulder. She stirred but did not wake.

**

When Cheryl woke, Adam was sitting up in bed watching her. He bent down to kiss the top of her head as she blinked away her grogginess. "Is it late?"

"No. I was up early. I couldn't sleep." She watched his face, trying to interpret the deepening lines on his forehead.

"What's wrong?"

"I think you're right. We should just go back to Florida." There was something in the way he looked at her that made her worry. He had changed his mind just when she had decided they should stay.

"I remember the house T.G. showed us. If we drive around, I think I can find it. We should--"

He didn't even let her finish. "Head home and let the police handle this."

She cocked her head at him. "I don't understand. Just last night, you said we had to do this. Now that I think I know where it is, you want to go home? That's not like you. That's what I do. You're the one who pushes us forward. What's going on?"

He looked off to the side, the way he did when he wanted to keep a secret. "You should get dressed."

"No. I'm not going to get dressed until you tell me what's going on. You're acting weird, and I don't like it. Tell me what happened. Did she show you something else last night?"

His jaw tensed. He stood and paced in front of the bed. She watched him walk back and forth a few times until he finally decided to speak. "I saw the house last night. T.G. showed me the house and..." His words trailed off.

"And what?" Cheryl already imagined the worst, not solving the crime and somehow both of them ending up dead.

"I went inside, and there were body parts everywhere." He stopped pacing and looked down at the floor. "It was gruesome. Bloody legs and arms and..." He looked up and gazed at her with his piercing eyes. "Cheryl, you were one of them."

"What? That's impossible. I'm right here." The idea sent chills down her spine. She pulled the blanket over her lap.

"It could be something that happens in the future."

Was that even possible? Cheryl had no idea. "I'm learning this as I go along just like you are now. I've never experienced anything like that before though." She wondered if he was suddenly becoming the one with the gift. "Tell me what else you saw."

"That's it. The house. The lake. I went inside, and I already told you that part. When I saw you, I fell into a puddle of blood. When..." He stopped. "I'm not sure how to talk about any of this. When I came back here, I had blood on me. Look." He went into the bathroom and came out holding a pair of light blue boxers with a large, dark red stain on them.

He reached out like he was handing them to her.

She shook her head. "I don't have to hold them." She saw that the fabric had stiffened where the stain was. "Did you hurt yourself last night?"

"No." He let out an exasperated sigh. "I fell in blood at the house."

She didn't want it to be true, but there was no explanation. She'd seen so many things that she couldn't explain that most people wouldn't believe. "So if we stay, Mark will kill me?"

"I don't know, but that's what it looks like." He sat on the bed next to her and put his arm around her shoulder.

"But what if what you saw happened because we left Mark out there to keep killing people? What if what you saw happened because we gave up and tried to run away?" It was all so confusing.

"I don't know, but I want to keep you as far away from him as possible." He tightened his grip on her shoulder, but she resisted her desire to melt into him.

"I think this is even more evidence that we need to keep going. We have to stop him." Her conviction surprised even her. Being in this town was painful, and the idea of finding Mark even more so. She had to believe she could help, do something to make all of this right. She was responsible. She had left him in the world to do so much damage and now look. And even though she ran away, there was a possibility that he could still get her. "I'm not running away anymore, Adam. I need to deal with this. If I stop Mark, it'll make me stronger than I ever even thought I could be. It will be good for us."

He seemed to be mulling the idea over, but before he could respond, she had more to say.

"The house is on the east side of town. I remember now. I went there with Mark once but didn't go inside. I just waited

Lady in the Lake

in the car while he went inside to get something. He was acting strange that day, jumpy." She remembered how angry he got that day. It was like everything she'd said was the wrong thing. "I don't know exactly what street it's on, but I think if we get into the general area, I'll figure it out. You know how I am. I don't pay attention when I'm not driving, but I'll recognize things."

"I know the house number, 4444. I saw it before I went inside." He pursed his lips and looked at the floor. "I don't think you should go there."

"How else can you find it? You need me there." She got up from the bed, walked over to the table, and picked up the crinkled note they'd found on the door the previous day. "I don't want to stay here alone after we got this."

"You've got a point," he said.

"Let me get dressed. We'll grab some food and head out there." Cheryl did her best to act nonchalant, but a feeling of doom gathered inside her like a dark cloud. She suspected that no matter what she did, she might end up one of the bodies in the house. Mark already knew she was here, and he obviously had plans for her.

Chapter 6

Cheryl always gave her stomach priority. It was a simple fact that Adam had gotten used to. Even catching a serial killer wasn't more important than having a proper breakfast. While he waited for her, he ran over the vision T.G. had shown him in his mind, searching for clues.

"Ready?" she asked, pulling her hair up into a messy ponytail. She said it like she had been waiting for him all along and not the other way around.

"I've been ready since six o'clock this morning." He picked up the keys, and they headed out.

Cold air punched him in the face as they stepped outside. The temperature had dropped considerably during the night.

"This is the other reason I moved." Cheryl zipped her coat and tucked her chin beneath the collar.

He wished he had a hat to keep his ears warm. He knew they were probably turning bright red from the cold. He pulled the motel door closed, and it beeped, alerting him that it had locked. As it did, he panicked. "I forgot to pick up the key." He checked his coat pockets.

"I've got it."

He turned around to look at her just in time to see a man in a gray suit rush up and grab her around the neck.

Cheryl yelled in terror before stomping on his foot and

Lady in the Lake

elbowing him in the gut. The man yelled, letting go to double over in pain. She spun around and kneed him in the face. Stunned, he took a few steps back, his nose bloodied. It didn't take long for him to regain his balance and charge her like a ferocious animal. Adam jumped between them and punched him. The man stumbled backward but didn't give up. Within a split second, he was launching himself forward again. Adam unleashed a series of punches, striking the man in the face and the upper body. He hadn't been in a physical fight since grade school. The idea of hitting someone with his bare hands would have normally made him shrink away, but he needed to protect Cheryl. The man fell onto his back on the blacktop, his arms up to protect his face.

"Who are you?" he yelled at the man.

The man didn't answer. Instead, he leaped to his feet and plowed past Adam to Cheryl, who was standing in front of the motel room door. She yelled as he knocked her into the wall. Adam grabbed him from behind and yanked him off of her. He was so wrapped up in what was happening that he didn't hear the police sirens. He didn't even know they had come until they were separating the three of them and putting them in handcuffs.

"Wait a minute," Cheryl protested. "We didn't do anything wrong. We were protecting ourselves."

"He attacked us." Adam wasn't sure the police would believe them, but then a woman came out of one of the motel rooms, her hair in pink rollers.

"I saw the whole thing out the window. He attacked them for nothing." She pointed at the man who was still bleeding from the mouth and nose.

"She's telling the truth. I saw it too." A man in a leather jacket and jeans came up to them. "I'm the one who called 911."

"All right, then," the stocky police officer with a 1970s-style mustache said. He took the handcuffs off Cheryl and Adam. "You still have to come to the station to give us a statement."

Adam went over to Cheryl and put an arm around her. "Are you okay?"

She nodded. "What do you think that was all about?"

"I don't know. You don't know him?" Adam had assumed he was Mark.

"I've never seen him before in my life." She glanced over at the man who wore a confused expression.

The man moved his arms, trying to pull his hands from the handcuffs. "What's going on? Why are you arresting me?" he asked the police. "What are you doing? I didn't do anything." The officers put him into the back of their cruiser as he yelled.

Adam looked with pity at the man who seemed genuinely confused. "He must be messed up. I wonder what he's on?"

Cheryl shrugged. "Does it matter?"

One of the officers approached them. He was wire-thin with a beak-like nose. "I'll take you downtown to get a statement."

They exchanged looks before agreeing to go. Adam figured they should file some kind of complaint. He didn't know what was wrong with the guy, but he was definitely dangerous if whatever he was taking made him act like that. It felt strange to get in the back of a police car though. "We'll meet you there."

The officer looked at both of them before giving a sharp nod. "All right." He got into his car and drove away.

"You put up some fight," Adam said to Cheryl as they drove to the police station.

"I guess all of the self-defense classes I took paid off."

Lady in the Lake

"They certainly did." He was glad to see that she could take care of herself. He often worried about her.

"After I left Mark, I made sure to take some classes. I never wanted to feel helpless again. That was the first time I used any of them though." He could see the pride in her eyes.

"You did good," he said. "I should hire you to be my bodyguard."

She chuckled. "Like you need a bodyguard."

Adam's hand ached from the fight. He could already feel his knuckles beginning to swell. They turned up the road by the police station. Once they got this statement out of their way, they could get back to looking for the house that T.G. had shown them and solving her case.

**

Cheryl was not thrilled to be back in the police station, and this time with an empty stomach. When she noticed Detective Haskell eying them as they walked across the station, she felt even less enthusiastic.

"Wait here," the officer said as he deposited them into an all-too-familiar dreary room.

They sat down, and Detective Haskell stuck his head in the door. "Back again?"

Cheryl couldn't help herself. "We missed your smiling face."

Adam gave her a sideways glance, but she didn't care.

"So you've got another hot tip for us?" Detective Haskell snickered.

"Not that it's any of your business, but someone assaulted me outside our motel room. We're here to give a statement." He didn't deserve to know anything about why they were there.

Adam elbowed her. "We'll be out of here soon."

Detective Haskell shook his head as he stepped out of the room.

"Behave yourself. We want to keep the police on our side." Adam pulled his phone from his pocket and set it on the table. His knuckles were turning purple.

"They should give you some ice for your hand." She reached out and took his hand in hers gently. "Do you think you broke something?"

"It isn't that bad." He shrugged.

"I'll go ask them for some ice." She started to stand.

"Don't. It's fine. Let's just make our statements and get out of here." He looked worried.

"It's going to be okay." She was reassuring him, but she didn't believe it herself. Logic told her that the man who attacked her was insane or high or both. He could've attacked anyone on the street, but it felt personal. Was he looking for her specifically?

"I'm afraid that every minute we're here, he's another minute closer..." Adam stopped.

"Closer to what?"

"I don't want you to end up dead."

She didn't want to end up dead either, but she didn't want anyone else to end up that way too. "I know. That's why we have to stop this. We'll give our statements, and then we'll look for the house." Her stomach growled. "First, we'll eat. Then we'll look for the house."

A small blonde police officer with a crooked face came into the room. She set a recorder down on the table. "I'm Officer Garfunkel." She shook both of their hands. "I just need you to tell me exactly what happened, and then we'll send you on your way." She sat down in the chair across from

Lady in the Lake

Cheryl. "Your attacker says he doesn't remember anything at all. He has no idea why he's even here. We'll be testing him for narcotics." She reached forward and pushed record on the device she'd placed on the table. "Let's talk about what happened this morning."

They told the officer what happened, each of them taking turns sharing what they remembered. It had all happened so fast that it was hard to get all the details right.

"I can't believe he doesn't remember any of it. He was so focused on me. It wasn't like he would've lashed out at just anyone. It felt like he was going after me specifically." Cheryl remembered the intense look in his eyes when he charged her.

"And you're sure you don't know him?" the officer asked.

Cheryl shook her head.

"If he is high, he could've been hallucinating." She stopped the recorder. "We've gotten everything we need from you." She clasped her hands in front of her on the table and looked at both of them.

Cheryl wasn't sure if she was expecting them to say something else. "So, we can go?"

Officer Garfunkel stood up and opened the door. "Go right ahead. We'll contact you if we need anything else from you."

Cheryl couldn't wait to get out of the station. She was starving.

**

Adam ordered a spicy pepper and onion omelet that he picked at as he jiggled his leg anxiously under the table. He couldn't understand how Cheryl seemed so calm. She even seemed happy as she bounced in her chair while she ate. His knuckles had only swelled a little, but they ached. His stomach was sour with worry.

She took her time with her meal. "You're not hungry?" She glanced at his plate.

"Don't you think we should hurry up and get out of here?" He looked at the front door of the restaurant. They seemed to be a magnet for unstable people since they'd arrived in town.

She wiped her mouth. "Here's what I think. The house will still be there, and so will T.G.'s body no matter when we start looking. I can't think straight if I don't eat. So I want to sit here and enjoy my breakfast because who knows what the rest of the day will be like." Her mouth curled into a devilish grin. "Who knows how many days I have left."

"That's not funny." He hated thinking of what his vision implied. He took a bite of his omelet. It wasn't great, but it wasn't terrible either. "Hopefully, the rest of the day will be better."

Cheryl chuckled. "If we do find Mark, it'll only be downhill from here. We could both end up dead. Unless..." She pulled a small bag of cream-colored powder from her coat pocket and put it on the table.

"What's that?" He reached out and took it in his hand. The powder was as fine as powdered sugar.

"Banishing powder. Day gave it to me before we left."

He handed the bag back to her. "Does it work?"

"If it doesn't, we're pretty screwed." Her gaze landed on something behind Adam, and pity clouded her expression.

"What's wrong?"

"Nothing. Just a ghost who looks so sad. I hope when we go to the other side, we're content. I don't want to spend my time hanging around holding onto regret. We could end up crossing over sooner rather than later."

Adam looked behind him and only saw a middle-aged woman eating a bowl of soup while reading a paperback. Her glasses perched on the end of her nose. He was hoping to be able to see more ghosts than just T.G. now. That wasn't the case. He turned back around to Cheryl. "You're not very reassuring." He choked down another bite of food.

"I'm honest. That counts for something." Too bad honesty wasn't enough to keep them safe.

Chapter 7

"Everything's starting to look the same. I'm not quite sure what road we should be on." Cheryl looked out the window as the trees and houses rolled by. It felt like they'd been driving around for a lot longer than they had. Now all the houses and all the streets looked so unfamiliar that she thought she would never be able to pick out the place. If she could just find a landmark, she'd know they were headed in the right direction.

"Are you sure we're on the right side of town?" Adam slowed at the stop sign. "We've been driving around this area for ages. Maybe we need to try somewhere else."

Cheryl shook her head. This was the right area. She knew it. "Why doesn't T.G. help us when we need it most?"

Adam shrugged before pulling off again. "You know more about how this works than me." He turned left up another wide street with rows of houses on either side. "I think we've been up every street in this neighborhood."

"I think you're right." As they continued to drive, the houses grew farther apart.

"Maybe I should just turn around, and we should go to a different neighborhood."

Every time he suggested going to a new neighborhood, Cheryl felt a little sick. She was convinced that meant something. "Not yet. I think we're close." She looked out the

Lady in the Lake

window at the trees and the occasional two-story wooden house. Cars sat in driveways. The trees had dropped their leaves, and their branches pointed aggressively at the overcast gray sky. When they passed a big clump of trees, Cheryl noticed something she hadn't before; a narrow road flanked by shrubbery. "Slow down. What's that?" She pointed.

Adam slowed down, and the car behind them rushed up to their bumper impatiently. "I don't know. Is that a driveway or a road?"

"Turn. Let's find out."

Adam turned the wheel, and the car skidded on to the street. "Sorry." The driver behind them leaned on the horn letting out a long beep.

"It's my fault. I told you to turn too late." They drove slowly up a narrow road only wide enough for a single car. On either side of them stood trees with papery gray bark. The car bounced through potholes. "I think this is the place."

"You think? It seems like if you'd been up this road before you'd remember."

She did remember. Mark had taken her here once on their way to the store. It was out of the way, but when she had asked him where they were going, he wouldn't answer. She knew not to complain. So she just sat in the passenger seat looking out the window, quietly daydreaming. "I remember. The road wasn't this messed up before. But I do remember."

The narrow road snaked through the trees. After about a mile, the trees opened up, and to the right, they saw the lake. Cheryl gasped, and Adam stopped the car. "That's it!" She opened the door and got out.

Adam did too. They left the car idling on the road as they crossed over the rocky ground between them and the lake. A layer of ice covered its surface. The scene was so much less sinister in the daylight.

"You think she's down there somewhere?" Adam asked, pulling Cheryl out of her thoughts.

"I think she's definitely down there. We need to call the police." She didn't want to have anything to do with the police anymore, but what other option did they have?

She looked at Adam who was standing by the lake looking up toward the pale yellow, two-story house with a crooked roof. "I'm going up there." Leaving the car in the middle of the road with the keys inside, Adam started walking through the meadow to the house.

"Don't. I don't think it's safe. I want to call the police first." Cheryl hurried after him grabbing hold of his arm.

"If he's there, I want to confront him." His voice was heavy with anger.

"Confront him and do what? You could end up getting killed."

He trudged forward, ignoring her.

"Let's get back in the car and call the police." Cheryl looked at Adam's shiny car sitting abandoned on the road. "Think of your vision. Evil lives in that house. We can't stand up to it alone." Nothing she said seemed to convince him. "Adam, I love you, and I'm not going to lose you to Mark. He's tried to take everything from me, and he's not taking you."

He stopped and turned around. "You love me?"

Cheryl nodded, and a tear slipped down her cheek. "Of course I do. I see everything you do for me, and I'm so grateful because nobody's ever treated me like that before. That's why sometimes I get all messed up, and I don't know what to do or how to act."

Adam rushed toward her and swept her up in his arms. Cheryl laughed, and they kissed. For a moment, she forgot about the evil that waited for them in the house only yards

Lady in the Lake

away. Cheryl even thought she heard birds singing somewhere in the distance. It didn't take long for the gravity of the situation to return. She linked her arm in his as they walked back to the car.

"If we call the police, what should we tell them?" Adam asked.

He had a point. They'd only been in town for two days, and this would be the third contact with the police. There was something amusing about that. Cheryl had spent all her time trying to avoid the police when she lived here, and now that she was visiting, they were becoming regulars in her life. "Let's talk to Detective Haskell. He might think we're crazy, but at least he knows who we are."

**

Adam didn't really expect Detective Haskell to show up. He was surprised when Cheryl got off the phone and said he was coming. "How did you do that?" he asked. He pulled the car off the road into the gravel just in case someone else happened along while they waited for the police. Someone did. A navy blue sedan ambled up the road. When it pulled up on the gravelly shoulder behind their car, the door swung open, and Detective Haskell got out.

He was alone. He wore a pair of navy pants and a black winter coat. He had a sallow complexion and the haggard look of an insomniac. He walked over to the lake and stood on the rocky edge looking in.

Adam and Cheryl got out of the car and joined him at the water's edge.

"So you think there's a body in here?" He picked up a rock and tossed it, sending it skittering across the ice.

"Yep," Cheryl said.

"And it's connected to the serial killer we're after?" He looked at her with suspicion in his eyes.

Adam had told her not to say it had anything to do with the serial killer because they didn't know if it had.

Detective Haskell looked at her for a long time as if trying to figure out if she was lying. "If there is, it should be easy to find." The lake was so small that it probably wasn't really a lake at all. "I think this is private property though. We can't search anything without the owner's permission."

"Even if the owners are murderers?" Cheryl asked.

"You don't know anything of the sort, do you?" Detective Haskell pulled his pack of cigarettes from his jacket pocket and lit up. After taking one long, satisfying drag, he opened his mouth to let the smoke curl out. "Let's drive up to the house and find out who lives there. Hopefully, whoever it is will give us permission to search this lake."

They followed him the rest of the way up the bumpy road to the house. When he got out of the car, Cheryl ran up to him. By the time Adam joined them, she was telling him about her ex and how dangerous he was. Detective Haskell didn't seem to take any of what she said seriously. "I'm going to knock and see what happens."

"I am telling you that someone dangerous lives in this house, and that he has killed a lot of people. Shouldn't you call for backup?"

Haskell took a puff of his cigarette before dropping it in the driveway and stomping it out. "This isn't a television show. This is real life, and you haven't given me any evidence that your ex-husband has killed anyone or that there's even really a body in this lake, so there's no reason for backup. These are probably just normal people living in this house, wondering why the heck we're here. I'm going to knock on the door and ask a few questions. That's the best I can do for now." He turned and walked up the path. Realizing they were following him, he said, "You two stay here, or better yet, wait in your car."

They didn't get in the car but instead stood at the end of the walk, where they had a clear view of the front door. Detective Haskell knocked, and Adam's body tensed. He half expected Mark to explode through the door in a fit of rage.

Mark didn't open the door. A round older woman with short, gray, curly hair did. She wore a bright red sweater and the kind of jeans that probably had an elastic waistband. She talked to Haskell for a while. Adam and Cheryl could not hear what they were saying. They could only imagine.

"I can't just stand here." Cheryl hurried up the walkway toward the detective and the woman. "Sorry." She held up her hand as she spoke like she was a student in the classroom. "Ma'am, you don't know me, but--"

Adam rushed up behind her. Haskell scowled.

Undeterred, Cheryl ignored both of them. "Do you know Mark Hampton? He's been here before. I'm his wife, and I came here with him once a few years ago."

The woman pursed her lips and shook her head. "Mark Hampton? It doesn't ring any bells. Is he in some kind of trouble? I don't know him. I don't have anything to do with him."

"But I was here. He went inside your house. Does anyone else live with you?"

"Just my husband." The woman turned her attention back to Haskell. "We haven't done anything wrong."

"I'm sorry about this, ma'am," Haskell said.

"Sorry? Why are you apologizing to someone who is implicated in murder?" Cheryl yelled.

"Murder?" The woman clutched her chest. Her mouth hung open in shock. "I didn't murder anyone."

"Okay, Cheryl." Adam put his arm around her waist. "This isn't going to get us anywhere." He turned her around, and they walked toward the car together.

"He can't get away with this. I can't let him do this to any more women." Her voice shook.

"We're not, but we don't know when what we saw happened. For all we know that woman just moved into this house last week."

"I doubt it," she said. "How long have you lived here?" Cheryl yelled over her shoulder at the woman.

"Almost thirty years now." The woman called back.

"See, she must be involved." Cheryl tried to pull away from him, but he tightened his grip around her waist.

"Okay. She might have been involved, but yelling at her about it while she stands at the front door isn't going to help anything." He kept his voice calm and steady as he walked her back toward the cars. He was relieved when she stopped fighting him.

"We can't let them get away."

"We're not going to." Once they reached the cars, they turned around to look back toward the house where Detective Haskell was still talking to the woman.

"She's got a lot to say. Do you think she's confessing?" Cheryl leaned her head against his chest.

He put his arm around her shoulders and squeezed her into him. He wished it could be that easy. "I doubt it."

Lady in the Lake

Chapter 8

The conversation looked far too amicable from a distance. Cheryl knew that when you were talking to a possible murderer, you shouldn't be that nice. At least she wouldn't have been, but she had to leave the detective work to the professionals. Detective Haskell must know what he's doing, right? Or did he?

When the woman closed the door, he turned and started back up the walkway. Cheryl couldn't believe it.

"Are you going to search the lake?" She broke free from Adam and met Detective Haskell halfway up the walkway.

He shook his head. "I can't do that."

"What do you mean you can't do that? I just told you there's a body in there." She pointed at the lake.

"What you told me doesn't matter if there's no evidence. There's no reason for me to get a warrant." His condescending tone aggravated her.

"I know you're the detective and all--" She began.

"Yes, I am." He pulled the pack of cigarettes from his pocket.

Cheryl tried her best not to roll her eyes. "And you know how to handle these things because of experience and all, but I have some information that I know for a fact is right. If you find this body and solve this case, think of how good it will make you look. You don't have to say anything to anyone about how you got the information. You can tell everybody that you were acting on a hunch, and that would be fine by us. Right, Adam?" She looked at him for support.

Adam agreed quickly. "The less I'm involved in all of this, the better."

She gave him a questioning look but decided against asking him what he meant.

Haskell held his unlit cigarette between his fingers, waving it around as he spoke. "That's not how things work around here. I'm not going to potentially ruin my reputation to put another notch in my belt. You need just cause to search someone's property; otherwise, you risk getting any evidence you do find thrown out."

"It won't take long. It's a small lake. What if there's a dead girl at the bottom, and you didn't even try to find her?" She glanced over at Adam again. Why wasn't he trying to convince the detective too?

"I don't have a missing person report. There's no evidence or witnesses that there was a crime of any sort. All I have is your word to go on, and frankly, that's not worth much. You came into town the other day and have been to the police station twice already. That's a red flag to me." He pulled out his lighter and lit his cigarette. A puff of smoke spiraled into the air.

"I don't know why you came out here, then. You knew who we were when we called. So what are you doing?" She was angry now.

"Let's go." Adam tugged on her arm. "We don't need his help to solve this case."

"Case?" Haskell sneered. "You two think you're on some kind of case. Are you cops now?"

Adam frowned. "What we are is none of your business."

"It certainly seems like it is since you called me." His cigarette hung from his lips, bouncing up and down as he spoke.

"Forget it." Cheryl turned to walk away. "Forget we called you. Forget all of it."

"We have to look into every tip that comes up about the Ridge Point Killer. Those are our orders. We don't know when something might sound crazy at first but turn out to be true." The gruffness in his voice faded. "This whole thing is running everybody at the department ragged."

Cheryl turned back around. For the first time, she noticed that he looked like he hadn't slept. His eyelids drooped, and dark circles marked the spaces beneath his eyes. "Why did you talk to her so long if you didn't think we were giving you good information?"

"She just asked me about the serial killer case. That's all anybody wants to talk about these days." He went over to his car.

"You're going?" Cheryl expected something more.

He looked at both of them. "If you can give me some evidence, a missing person report, a name, a witness. Anything solid. I'll look into it. Until then, leave me alone. There's a lot going on in this town, and I have work to do." He got into the car before Adam and Cheryl could respond.

Cheryl ran up to his car and knocked on the window. He rolled it down. "What if I can tell you that I know who's doing all this?"

He scowled. "This isn't a game. You can't run around pointing fingers at people with no evidence."

"Who said that I thought it was a game?"

He narrowed his eyes at her. "Go on then."

"Mark Hampton." She blurted the name out.

"You keep bringing him up. He must've been a pretty

rotten husband," he cocked his head at her.

"He's a violent guy." She knew what she was saying wasn't evidence, but she wanted to tell him. "He'd kill somebody if he got the chance."

"How do you know that?" He raised his chin.

"He almost killed me." Her voice caught in her throat.

"I'm sorry. He sounds like a terrible man, but beating your wife doesn't necessarily make you a serial killer." He looked into her eyes, and for a moment, Cheryl thought he might believe her. "If you get some solid evidence, call me. Until then, try to stay out of trouble." His car bounced down the thin, bumpy road.

They might have been on their own to solve the case, but Cheryl saw a hint of something in his eyes that let her know that if they did need his help in the future, Detective Haskell might be on their side.

**

"Cheryl, get in the car. We should go." Adam looked at the house where the woman had parted the curtains on the side window and stood watching them.

"I should've known that he wouldn't help us." She stood facing the trees and the lake, her hands hanging at her side.

"Let's go." He opened the passenger side of the car and led her to the door. She climbed in slowly, only half paying attention to her surroundings. "We need to find her body. We need to make sure Mark pays."

"I know." He got in the car and started the engine.

"If only we could find Mark and get him to confess."

Adam laughed. "That's a long shot."

"I know." She pulled her phone out of her purse.

"What are you doing?"

Lady in the Lake

"Looking for an article or something about a missing person with the initials T.G. We have to figure out who she was and what happened. We need some kind of evidence to show Haskell." She looked skyward and held out her hands. "You need to give us more solid information, or else we won't be able to help you."

"What are you doing?"

She turned her attention back to Adam. "Asking T.G. to give us better clues. I wish she would just talk to me again, so I can find out who she is."

"She'll tell one of us something when she's ready." Adam made the turn to drive back to their motel.

**

Large black letters painted on their motel room door were visible before they even got out of the car. "YOU STAY YOU DIE!" The spray paint read.

Mark had found her. Cheryl knew this was his work. Who else could it be? "He's found me." Cheryl began to shake. "He left the note and now this." She looked out the car window searching for him in the parking lot.

Adam got out of the car and walked up to the door. As he did, a squat, balding man came up to him.

"Get out!" The man pointed at Adam. "I don't know who's after you, but I don't want any trouble in my motel."

"Did you see who did this?" Adam asked, pointing at the spray-painted door.

The manager shook his head. "It doesn't matter who did it. You're paying for it."

The woman in the room next to theirs poked her head out of the door. Her hair was perpetually in pink foam rollers. She had a red bandanna tied over it. "I saw what happened. A junkie did it. He was laughing like a crazy person. When he saw me, he took off, running across the street right in front of all the traffic. It was a miracle that nobody ran him over."

"Do you know him?" Adam asked.

"Do I look like I hang out with junkies to you?" She shook her head at him.

"No. I was wondering if he looked familiar to you." The last thing Adam wanted to do was get on her bad side.

"I might've seen him on the main drag, all doped up and asking people for money." She shifted her attention to the manager. "Arnie, you can't make these kids pay for that. They don't have any control of what some junkie does."

"Shut up, Sylvia. It's my motel, and I'll run it the way I see fit." He pointed his finger at Adam again. "You get out of here. I don't want to see your face around here again."

"She just told you what happened. We didn't have anything to do with it."

"I said you better get out of here. Leave now, and I won't make you pay for the damages." It was like he was this broken record.

"We paid for two more nights." Adam examined the spray paint dripping down the door. The letters even looked aggressive.

"Get out now or I'll call the police." His face reddened.

Adam stood in front of him defiantly. "Good. Call the police then." He didn't really want to deal with the police again, but he hated being treated unjustly. "You can't kick us out without giving us our money back."

"I'm the owner. I can do whatever I want." He started marching back up to the office. Then he spun around and said, "Clear your stuff out of that room and get out of here. You got twenty minutes. Then I'm calling the police."

Chapter 9

"That place was a dump anyway." Cheryl sat back in her seat. They'd gathered their things up quickly and left without trying to get a refund.

"You booked it." Adam had been surprised when they first pulled up to the rundown motel.

"I don't remember the area being that bad, and the place looked okay online. I should've known though. Anything that cheap was bound to be a bad idea." The quality of the motel didn't matter much now. They weren't going to be staying there anymore, and she was relieved. She knew the threat painted on the door and the note they'd gotten the day before were both meant for her. Mark knew she was there. She didn't know where he was, but he knew where she was. That gave him all the power. She couldn't have that. She was scared, but she wanted to make sure he never found out how scared she really was. "I talked to Sylvia before we left."

"Yeah, I saw that," he said.

"I asked her about the junkie she saw. I think it might be Mark." The man Sylvia had described sounded older than Mark, but Cheryl knew that drug use aged you. She had watched one of her college friends become a hollow husk of a person as she surrendered to the chains of addiction. "We should drive around downtown and look for him."

They drove in circles around the sleepy downtown area. The only people outside were the ones hurrying between stores and their parked cars. Small mounds of snow, black and gray from pollution, were piled beside sidewalks. In many ways, it was like Cheryl had never left Ridge Point, but even though the remnants of who she once was haunted her, she was a completely different person now. She kept reminding herself of all she'd accomplished since leaving Ridge Point. She'd started a whole new life from scratch with nothing but a few dollars and the clothes on her back. Somehow she'd manage to land on her feet, and she was thankful for that every day.

She spotted a man wrapped in a tattered jacket standing on the corner in front of the pharmacy. His back faced them, but he was the same height as Mark. There was something in the way he swayed back and forth as he stood looking at the wall that reminded her of him. "Pullover." Her heart raced.

Adam pulled the car into the empty parking space nearby. "Is that him?" He looked in the same direction as Cheryl.

"I think so."

Adam turned off the car and jumped out. "Wait here." He slammed the door.

She couldn't wait. She put her hand in her coat pocket and felt the smooth plastic of the baggie of banishing powder there. She needed to make sure it was really him. This could be it. It could be her chance to get rid of him once and for all. She got out and followed him up the slushy sidewalk, her feet getting wet in her tennis shoes.

"Hey! Hey, you!" Adam yelled.

Cheryl could feel his anger, and part of her wanted to recoil from it. She was angry too, but she didn't want a fight.

The man whirled around to face them. "What can I do you for?" he slurred, revealing a toothless grin. Cheryl's heart

Lady in the Lake

sank. She thought this would be it. "It's not him." She rushed forward, slipping in the slush and grabbed Adam's arm to keep herself upright.

"Are you sure?" Adam whispered.

"It's not him." They turned around, quickly marching away from him as if nothing had happened.

"I can be anybody you want me to be." The man called after them as they walked away.

Cheryl pulled the car door closed. "I was hoping that was him."

"I know. I was too." Adam started the car.

She pointed straight in front of them. "Up here, about six blocks, there's a bar Mark used to hang out in. Maybe someone there will know where we can find him."

He pulled out of the parking space. "Let me know when we get close."

She nodded, looking out the window. "It's crazy how I'm kind of trying to avoid Mark while looking for him at the same time."

"Yeah."

She watched drab brick-faced buildings that made up much of downtown pass by through the passenger window. "Slow down. It's just up here," she said as they approached the block that contained Mark's favorite bar. She remembered how often he'd come home from there stumbling drunk and fueled by anger.

Adam slowed down. "Where?"

The building that once housed Cody's Bar was abandoned. Boards covered the windows, and a thick chain hung on the door. The sign across the top of the low building hung at an angle like it might fall off at any moment.

"Well, it looks like that's closed." He'd pulled over into a parking space in front of the building.

"I can't believe this." She pulled her phone from her bag and looked at the blank screen. If only she knew someone she could call to ask about where Mark was these days, but there was no one. He never introduced her to his friends, and he didn't have any family. No one that she knew about anyway. "I'm stuck. I can't believe I was married to him, and I don't know anyone I can call to find out where he is now."

Her phone dinged.

"Text?" Adam asked.

She read the message. "Yeah, it's just Stephanie." Stephanie was the first friend she made when she moved to St. Pete.

When are you back in town? Something weird is going on.

She quickly typed out a response. *Don't know. Why? What's up?* She watched the screen waiting to see if Stephanie was typing a response. When she didn't, she stuck the phone back in her bag.

"What's up with Stephanie?" Adam had pulled back out onto the road.

"I don't know. She didn't really say."

They stopped at a Chinese restaurant for dinner, to regroup and figure out what to do next.

"I don't understand how he knows I'm in town, but I can't find him anywhere?" Cheryl took a sip of water.

"He could've seen us somewhere and followed us back to the motel." Adam scanned the menu.

His explanation, while logical, didn't sit right with her. Mark had never been calculated enough to do something like that. He was all explosive emotions. It was much more likely for him to have run after her and threaten her life as soon as he saw her. "Why the messages though? If he knows I'm here, why not approach me? He loves the idea of making someone pay." She remembered all the times she'd seen him be unkind and even hostile to strangers for petty reasons.

"I don't know. I never met him." He closed his menu and set it aside. "Maybe he likes the idea of scaring you."

He did like to scare her, there were no maybes about it, but it still didn't make sense to her. "He doesn't have the patience for something like this though. He likes a direct attack. He doesn't want to wait around and watch someone squirm."

"He might've changed."

"That's doubtful." She sighed. "Looking back on my time with him, I can see so many clues to the monster he became. I was out of my mind with love when I decided to marry him." She shook her head. "That was one of the worst decisions I've ever made. I still feel like I can't trust myself."

"It's always easier to see the clues in retrospect. You're not the only one who's ever married the wrong person."

Cheryl knew this, but hearing it from someone else made her feel a bit better. She'd made a mistake, and it was time to forgive herself and move on. She hoped that finding Mark and solving T.G.'s case would help her do just that. She took out her phone while they waited for their food to arrive. "I'm going to look up local missing person's cases. Maybe I'll find something." She pulled up the local newspaper's website, and the headline on the homepage smacked her in the face. "He killed someone else." She held the phone up to Adam, who took it from her and read the headline out loud.

"Ridge Point Serial Killer Strikes Again."

The waiter came over and sat their food in front of them, but neither of them had much of an appetite now.

She scanned the article, relaying the most important information to Adam. "It says they found the body of a twenty-six-year-old woman who had been missing for five days buried in a park. Someone's dog dug her up." She passed the phone to him, too horrified to read any further.

She watched his face as he read the article, the creases between his eyes deepening, the light reflecting from his glasses. "It says there are still no suspects in the case." He put the phone down on the table. "We know who did it, but they won't listen to us."

He kept talking, but Cheryl didn't hear anything he said. She felt like she was coming apart. How many more women would die before she'd be able to stop Mark? She couldn't afford to wait around to find out.

"We can't sit here feeling helpless." Adam passed her phone back to her. "Let's search for missing person's cases like you started doing. The faster we can find some clues, the faster we can stop this."

They scrolled through old missing person's reports in the local newspapers. They'd each decided to search a different publication to see if they could find something about their ghost. They'd been sitting in the restaurant for more than an hour with their food still untouched, growing cold in front of them.

"I think this is it," Adam said suddenly. He slid his phone across the table to Cheryl. The picture in the article already told her that this was the woman they were looking for.

"Tanya Garrett disappeared in mid-July almost two years ago." She read the article. "She's from Somerset. That's almost three hours from here." She continued to read. "There's an interview with her mother, Anne Wilcox." Cheryl looked up from the phone. "We need to talk to her."

"It looks like we're going to Somerset." Adam raised his hand to get the waiter's attention.

**

Anne Wilcox's number wasn't hard to find, and initially, she sounded more exhausted than excited at the mention of her daughter's name.

"Who are you again? Are you with the police?" she asked.

Not sure how to respond, Cheryl told her that she was a psychic who was working with the police in Ridge Point.

"They're still investigating Tanya's case? I've been on them to keep looking, but it seemed like they stopped ages ago. I'm so glad they're still trying to find her." The joy in her voice unnerved Cheryl. "I'll answer any questions you have. If you need to look through her things, you can. I haven't touched her room in case there are clues there. I'll do whatever I can to get Tanya back."

Cheryl realized that Anne thought her daughter was still alive. Why wouldn't she? She got Anne to agree to meet them, but once she hung up, she regretted the whole conversation.

"She thinks she's still alive." Cheryl returned her phone to her purse.

"How should we tell her?" They already started the drive to Somerset before Cheryl had even called. The roads were relatively empty. Cheryl had been to Somerset before and knew that it would be an easy drive. The flat, monotonous scenery stretched as far as the eye could see.

Anxiety rose from her stomach up to her throat. "I don't know how to tell her."

"You've had enough practice."

"But it never gets any easier. With all the articles written about her, I don't see how her mother could still think she's alive. It seems so obvious." Of course, Anne didn't want to give up hope. Cheryl had been so wrapped up in her own fears and anxiety about looking for Mark that when she called Anne, she hadn't even considered that she might think her daughter was still alive. Wasn't it natural for a parent to try to hang on to that kind of hope?

"I can't imagine what she must have gone through." Adam remembered when his parents died. He held fast to the idea that they would come back one day, even though he knew it was impossible.

"Neither can I." The seriousness of what she had to do anchored her. Tanya would show up soon, and Cheryl would have to be a conduit for her to speak to her mother again. That kind of work always drained her, but it was the most important work she did.

They spent much of the drive in silence. Cheryl rehearsed the best words to say to tell Anne that her daughter was gone forever. She wanted every syllable to be just right.

When they got to Somerset, they went directly to Anne's white two-story house. A sprinkling of snow began to fall as they glided into the driveway. Adam put the car in park, and they sat with the motor running for a few moments looking at the house. It looked abandoned from the outside. A discarded newspaper lay on the front step next to a stack of terracotta flowerpots. A huge chip was missing from the top one in the stack. Dark gray grime on the windowsills peaked out from beneath the freshly fallen snow.

Cheryl took a deep breath. "Here we go." When she got out of the car, she saw Tanya standing on the front porch in her yellow floral dress. The cotton fabric stuck to her frame. Her dark hair hung in clumps from her scalp. "She's here." Cheryl pointed at the porch.

"Is she? Why can't I see her?" Adam squinted.

Cheryl laughed. "Squinting won't help."

They joined Tanya at the front door. "Is there something you want me to tell your mother?" Cheryl asked her.

She silently looked down at her bare feet. Water dripped

from her hair.

"You never were a big talker," Cheryl said.

She looked at Adam, who nodded before she rang the bell. The deep bark of what sounded like an enormous dog answered the chime of the doorbell. "Well, at least we know the dog's home."

"Too bad the dog can't give us any clues."

She rang the bell again.

The shadow of the dog, moving back and forth, appeared in the frosted glass door.

"It looks like it's about the size of a horse," Adam said.

Cheryl shuddered at the thought of the large furry dog jumping on her, teeth exposed, and devouring her from the inside out. She was so lost in this horrible scenario that she didn't even realize Anne Wilcox was coming to the door. She admonished the dog with a "Charlie, stop it!" And the great beast clopped off to some other area of the house. She swung the door open wide, and as soon as her face appeared in the doorway, Tanya Garrett began to cry. A stream of emotions rushed in so quickly that Cheryl felt like she was drowning. Her legs gave out, and Adam reached out to catch her. After that, everything went black.

Chapter 10

Adam caught Cheryl before he was even conscious that she was falling.

Anne Wilcox stood at her front door wearing a pair of jeans and an oversized button-shirt looking stunned. "Oh, no! Is she okay?"

"I'm sorry. This happens sometimes," he said.

The dog ran back toward the doorway and began to bark. A long string of drool hung from its mouth.

"Stop it, Charlie. Get!" She pointed off to the side, and Charlie looked up at her with large, brown eyes before hurrying back to the other room, his nails clicking on the wood floor.

"Bring her inside. It's freezing out there." She motioned for Adam to carry Cheryl in.

Adam hoisted her into his arms and carried her into the warmth of the house. Her arms hung limply, but her hands twitched, her fingers fluttering as if tapping out a rhythm.

"This way." Anne led them into a cozy living room. A worn oriental rug lay on the floor. A navy blue sofa flanked one wall beneath a large window. "Put her there." She pointed to the sofa.

Adam put Cheryl down. Before he'd even moved his arms out from under her, Anne placed a soft blanket over her.

Lady in the Lake

Cheryl's limbs twitched.

"Should I call an ambulance?" Anne asked.

"No, she'll be fine."

"She doesn't look fine to me." Anne stared down at Cheryl, who lay with her lids half-closed exposing the whites of her eyes.

The dog came in and trotted right up to the sofa to sniff Cheryl's twitching hand. It didn't take long for him to become distracted by something in the corner of the room. He growled at first, a low snarl that came from someplace deep within. His lips curled, showing his sharp white teeth. Then he began to bark. The noise echoed around the room, the fur on his haunches stood on end. He moved forward a bit, then backed up, unsure.

"Charlie, stop it," Anne demanded.

The dog ignored her and continued to bark at the corner.

Frustrated, she went over to him and grabbed his collar. She disappeared down the hallway. Adam heard a door open and close. "Stay in there," she said before coming back down the hall to join Adam. "I'm sorry he doesn't usually act like that."

"Don't worry about it." Adam was too worried about Cheryl to think about much else.

"I'm assuming that she's the psychic that called me earlier."

Adam remembered they hadn't even introduced themselves before Cheryl had passed out. He cleared his throat. "Yeah. I am her partner. My name's Adam."

"I'm Anne, but I'm sure you know that already." Even in this unusual situation, she had a comfortable demeanor.

It was difficult for him to take his eyes off Cheryl, but he did manage to glance at Anne. "I'm here to help out when stuff like this happens. I make sure she stays safe."

"So this happens a lot?" Anne's forehead creased. "I feel like I should call 911."

"She'll be fine. This happens all the time." He was trying to be reassuring, but every time he saw her like this, he had to fight the instinct to rush her to a hospital.

"Why?"

"It's kind of like a trance that she goes into when ghosts are telling her something emotional." That was the way she'd explained it to him in the past, and it seemed like the best explanation he could give.

"A ghost? You're telling me there's a ghost in her?"

Adam wondered how much he should say. "Cheryl told you about why we're here, right?" He didn't really have to ask this question because he'd heard the call.

"She said she was working on my daughter's case. She's been gone almost two years now." She bit her lip and looked at the floor. "I know that's not good. Usually, when someone has been gone that long, it's not good news, but I like to stay hopeful, you know. I realize that she's probably..." Her words trailed off.

Adam swallowed hard. "This might sound crazy to you, but Cheryl can talk to ghosts. She helps them find closure in this world so they can move on to the next." He was sure Anne was going to kick them out of her house, whether or not Cheryl seemed to be having a seizure.

"So, she sees dead people like the kid in <u>The Sixth Sense</u>." She chuckled.

"Kind of."

She grew quiet. He prepared himself mentally for the anger or ridicule that might follow, but instead, she told him a story.

"My nan lived to be a hundred. I still remember visiting her with my mom as a kid. She terrified me, but I never told

Lady in the Lake

anybody because I knew I wasn't supposed to be afraid of her. She was a strong-willed lady, and when she grabbed hold of my hand, she'd squeeze it so hard it felt like she might crush it. If I got too close to her, she'd grab my arm and just hold and squeeze, her bony fingers digging into my flesh. I'd hold back my tears because if I cried, my mother would get mad. Nan always said she could see her husband and her mother in her room. She would talk to them sometimes while we sat with her. My mother told me she was seeing people who weren't there because she was so sick that her mind was going, but I never thought that was true. If we could visit her, why couldn't family on the other side visit her too? She was hanging out between both worlds, waiting to cross over. People who loved her from the other side went to comfort her just like we did." She looked at Adam for a good long while with her vivid green eyes. "You can tell me whatever you need to tell me. I've been living with this for so long that I've imagined every possible scenario. I'm even ready to hear the worst."

Adam began from the beginning when he first saw Tanya. He explained everything they knew, which wasn't much really. They stood next to the sofa, watching Cheryl as he spoke. Anne didn't say much.

When Adam was done, she said, "I kind of knew she was dead all along. I felt it. She would never stay away for this long without calling. I didn't want to believe it, but I knew." A large tear ran down her face, and she wiped it away. "Pardon me for a minute." She rushed from the room before Adam could say anything else.

He squatted down next to Cheryl, watching her. Her eyes moved back and forth beneath her eyelids. Her head shook from side to side, and her lips moved ever so slightly. He wondered what was happening. What terrible things she was seeing? It was at times like this that he wished he could take her place.

He could hear Anne's loud gasping sobs floating in from another room. Eventually, the crying had stopped, but she was still somewhere else in the house when Cheryl finally returned to them.

**

Seeing her mother was a bit too much. As soon as the door swung open, Tanya gripped Cheryl. Reality fell away, and the world became something completely different. Cheryl crawled into Tanya's past.

**

"My turn was back there," Tanya said, craning her neck to look behind them as her street grew further and further away. The interior of the truck was dark gray. The fabric on the seats was torn in places, letting the yellowing foam peak through. A wide crack ran the length of the dashboard. The glove box refused to close. Instead, it gaped open, clattering each time they hit a bump, striking her knees. The seatbelt squeezed at her throat, and she used her hand to pull it away. The car smelled of stale cigarette smoke, and the sweet lingering scent of alcohol came from the partially empty beer cans behind the seat. They rattled as the truck rushed up the road. Tanya had an increasing feeling of dread gathering somewhere at the base of her throat. She looked down at her lap as if afraid to look at the driver and said, "I thought you were going to drop me off at home."

"There's something I gotta do first." His voice was a rumble, the words strung together as one.

"But I'm staying just back there. Coming back will be out of your way." She watched the wide road. Heat rose from the blacktop. The sky was clear, the sun a bright ball of yellow. She'd worn her favorite yellow dress because he had said they were going on a picnic, but the picnic consisted of nothing more than some Budweisers and a stale baguette he got from God knows where. She didn't know why she had expected more. She wasn't as gracious as she should be. He told her that a lot, and it was true. She was spoiled and expected too much. She should've been happy with what she had, and she sure was lucky to have him. No other guy had stayed with her this long. They all got bored so easily and moved on to someone else. He always came back even when she was difficult and even though she always said the wrong thing.

Tanya was going to be an actress. When she decided to run off to Hollywood, she thought she'd get further than a few hours from her stinking hometown, but she'd met him. He was so nice at first, almost too good to be true.

"What do you have to do?" She knew she was along for the ride, whether she wanted to be or not. Instead of stressing out because things hadn't gone exactly as planned, she was trying to learn to relax and go with the flow.

"You didn't think that picnic was all there was for your birthday, did you?" His voice lightened. "There's more."

"What?" She hadn't dared ask for a real present.

"I can't tell you. It's a surprise."

She used to hate surprises. When he said the word, her chest tightened a little, and she felt the anxiety creeping in, but she exhaled just like she'd been teaching herself to do. She breathed out the tension and forced a smile. "Great. I love surprises," she lied, hoping that whatever it was would be something good. Something better than stale bread and sex in the park on the dirty blanket he'd pulled from the truck bed. "Give me a hint so I can try to guess what it is." She hoped that a clue would make her a bit less anxious.

He shook his head and reached his hand over the gap between them to grip her thigh. His fingertips pressed into her soft flesh. "You'll see when we get there."

She was beginning to feel nauseous, so she cracked the window.

"Hey, I got the air conditioner in this thing charged for you. You don't like it." He sneered. His mood could turn so quickly.

"Ah, no. I'm just feeling a bit sick. Motion sickness maybe." She leaned forward as far as the open glove box would allow. "Could you pull over for a minute?" Everything around her began to spin. She grabbed hold of the door. The world rocked and spun. The truck turned a corner so quickly that she felt like she was on a bad amusement park ride. She groaned. She didn't want to, but she couldn't help herself. Her stomach did somersaults. She thought when he made the turn that he was pulling over, but instead they started up a bumpy road. She sat up slowly to see where they were and saw a very narrow road only large enough for one car at a time. It twisted through the trees. "Where are we going?"

He didn't answer.

"Hey, where are we going? What's the surprise? I really feel like I'm going to be sick. I think I need to go home." Her face felt as if it was going numb. Her tongue became floppy, and she didn't know if her words came out as words at all. Her eyelids drooped until it took all the strength she had to keep them open. Then the world went black.

When she woke, she couldn't open her eyes any further than narrow slits to see just the blurry suggestions of shapes, but she could feel what was going on around her. He jostled her. The car door swung open. He leaned over and unhooked her seat belt, and she felt herself being lifted out of the car and carried through the heavy humid heat. She tried to move her arms and legs, but they flopped limply as he walked with her. She tried to open her eyes to see where she was. The colors and shapes didn't make sense. Her brain worked in slow motion, her thoughts caught in mud.

Sometimes there was only darkness. Other times she was vaguely aware of movement around her. There were people, a lot of people. Sometimes they talked like at a party, the words a wave of sound. Other times in unison like a ceremony performed in church, the rise and fall of choral singing. He was there, standing over her most of the time. She could feel him.

She didn't know how long she was unconscious, but she did remember waking up. She lay on the floor in a room with candles lit all around her. Her head pounding, she tried to sit up, but it was difficult. Her stomach hurt. Her entire body ached. When she looked around in the candlelight, she saw him sitting in a chair watching her. She opened her mouth to speak but was unsure if she'd be able to say anything because her mouth was so cottony and thick. Her tongue felt swollen. She tried to choke out the words, but they were like wool. Picking up a glass of water from the table next to his chair, he leaned forward, handing it to her.

She took it and drank. The cool liquid slid down her throat. When she was finished drinking, she placed the glass on the floor beside her, and her eyes met his. "What did you do to me?" she demanded.

"Nothing you didn't deserve." His voice was like a club. A smirk slid across his face, and she suddenly saw him for the monster he was.

Tanya had been afraid before, plenty of times, but nothing

had prepared her for the absolute terror that lit up inside of her. She knew she had to leave. She knew that if she did not, she would pay with her life. Even though her body was still weak, her head still muddled, her eyes groggy, she was suddenly overcome with adrenaline. She had the power to move and move quickly, and she did. Somewhere in her, she summoned the strength to jump to her feet. She expected him to jump up too, but he didn't. He sat in the chair, watching her fumble with the chain lock and then the deadbolt. Her heart raced. He got up and walked toward her. Why weren't her fingers working? Finally, she unlocked the door and pulled it open. He tackled her from behind, knocking the wind out of her as they tumbled out the door. With him still on her back, she fell off the porch onto the lawn. Tanya ripped at the grass, trying to escape. Adrenaline numbed her from the pain she should've been feeling. She had to escape. She twisted around and punched him. Somehow she was able to break free. She launched herself across the lawn toward the trees. When he caught up with her, he punched her in the back. She crumpled to the ground like a rag doll. She cursed herself for being so weak. How could she have been so stupid to let this happen to her? He grabbed her under the armpits and dragged her through the grass. Her sandals slipped off.

"You think you could run so easily. You think you can leave me like she did. Once this is done, I'll be invincible, then what will you do?"

When her body hit the water, strength rushed into her again. Gasping, she fought, her hands flailing about trying to strike him but just striking the surface of the water again and again until her fist made contact with something solid. He yelped with pain.

"No! No!" She found her voice again, and it was loud and shrill and unwilling to be silenced.

Lady in the Lake

"Stop it!" he yelled.

"Help! Help!" she thought she saw someone. A silhouette in the trees, but they crouched down, hoping not to be seen instead of rushing to her rescue. The world had betrayed her. Her life was nothing to anyone--those were her thoughts before his hand pushed the top of her head, forcing her under.

Chapter 11

Cheryl gasped for air as panic rushed through her. Her eyes flew open, and she was relieved to see that she was not drowning in a murky body of water. She was lying on a couch in an unfamiliar living room.

Adam reached out his hand and placed it on her shoulder. "It's okay. Relax."

She blinked away her tears and focused on his face.

"Are you okay? What happened?" He sat on the floor next to her, his face close to hers.

"I was there. I know what happened. There was some kind of ritual." She tried to pull the memory of what she'd experienced back into her mind, but it was hazy.

"You saw Mark?" Adam asked.

"I think so." Her head hurt.

"What do you mean? Was it someone else?" His blue eyes searched her face.

"I don't know. It could've been Mark, but his face was a blur, and his voice was distorted. It was like I was experiencing everything through a filter." She tried to replay the car ride in her mind and the conversation she'd had with the killer but kept going back to those terrifying last few moments Tanya had fighting for her life. She began to shake, knowing that she'd suffered so much.

Lady in the Lake

"You're okay." Adam squeezed her shoulder. "You're here now."

"Who is Mark?" Cheryl hadn't even noticed Anne Wilcox standing behind Adam.

"I'm sorry." Cheryl glanced up at Anne.

"Don't apologize. I've been waiting for two years to find out what happened to my daughter. Tell me." Her face tensed, and she blinked quickly, holding back tears. "Tell me, so I can stop wondering and searching." A tear slipped down Anne's cheek. She wiped it away. "Who is Mark? Did he take my daughter away from me?" She sunk into the chair across from the couch. Her face pale with grief.

Her eyes jumped nervously to Adam, who answered the question. "We think so."

Anne pressed her lips together and looked at the floor.

A lump rose in Cheryl's throat. She couldn't imagine what Anne was feeling. "What did you know about her life before she disappeared?" Cheryl formed every syllable carefully.

"She's definitely dead, then?" Anne's voice quivered.

"I'm so sorry." Adam turned around to look at her.

"And you think this Mark person killed her?" Anne waited for an answer.

Both Cheryl and Adam nodded.

They sat in silence for a moment, each of them looking at the floor. Then Anne began to speak. "She moved out three months before she disappeared. She just up and left one day with a small bag of things. She'd left most of her stuff here, so I always assumed she was coming back for it." She looked off into the distance. "We didn't talk much. She called occasionally, but she wasn't interested in telling me what was going on with her. I didn't even know where she was living. I knew she was staying with friends, but that was it." She looked at Cheryl with sincerity in her eyes. "If I'd known where she was staying back then, I would've gone to see her. I love my daughter."

"You don't have to convince us of that. We're not here to put you on trial. We're here to help Tanya find justice and some peace," Adam said.

"I know." She paused. "She wanted to move to LA and become a movie star. She's beautiful and talented, but she never understood how tough life could be. I guess that was my fault. I spoiled her when she was little." A glint of memory shone in Anne's eyes. "She didn't realize how few people actually make it in Hollywood. I encouraged her to have a sensible backup plan, but she's always been a dreamer." A hint of a smile crept across her face. "That's my Tanya. Always dreaming." The serious look returned. "I wasn't trying to break her dreams. I just wanted her to be safe." She put her hand over her mouth and choked back a sob.

"Of course," Adam said.

"Sometimes, parents have to be the bad guys. It's my responsibility to guide her. I have the experience. I know what's really possible. It's wrong to tell your kids they can do anything when that's not the case." She stared down at her lap for a moment, her face freezing. Then without warning, she started up again. "I'm not a bad mother."

"Nobody said you were." Cheryl eased herself up to a seated position.

"I'm just making sure you don't misunderstand. I wasn't trying to squash her dreams." She pursed her lips, deepening the creases around her mouth. "You said you're working with the police."

Adam cleared his throat. Before he could say anything, Cheryl answered, "Yes."

Anne sat forward in her chair. "Why did they decide to start looking for her again?"

Lady in the Lake

"I'm not sure." Cheryl's speech slowed as she noticed Tanya appear in the far corner of the living room. Her pale face was no longer drawn with pain. Cheryl swore she could see peace in her eyes.

"Have they arrested this Mark person?" Anne sat forward in her chair.

Cheryl wanted more than anything to give her good news, but she had none. She shook her head. "I'm trying to get some definite evidence together so they'll pick him up." Her gaze flitted over to the corner of the room where Tanya stood. A light seemed to illuminate her.

Cheryl swallowed her emotions. "I think Tanya's murder is connected to the serial killer case in Ridge Point." Her words dropped like a stone to the floor.

"You think she was murdered by that serial killer?" Anne's face twisted with grief. She pulled a tissue from her pocket and wiped her nose.

Adam looked at Cheryl and then back to Anne. "We're so sorry that we have to be the ones to tell you."

She nodded. "Pardon me." She stood and rushed from the room again.

Cheryl and Adam sat together uncomfortably, listening to her sob loudly in the next room.

"No! No! Not my Tanya!" She wailed.

Cheryl wondered if they should go. Tanya disappeared from the corner. Then reappeared on the couch next to them. Adam jumped and grabbed hold of his heart. "When did you get there?"

"You can see her too?" Cheryl asked.

"Yeah," he said.

"Tell her I'm sorry. Tell her that I love her." Tanya shared her list of requests. Cheryl was used to this. It was what all the ghosts did.

85

"Is she saying something?" Adam asked.

"You can't hear that?"

Adam shook his head. "She's moving her mouth, but I can't hear anything."

"Interesting." Cheryl was curious about how their experiences with Tanya were different.

It wasn't long before Anne came back into the room. Her feet had become heavy beneath the weight of her sorrow.

Adam hopped up. "I wish we had better news to tell you. We are doing our best to catch her killer."

"I kind of knew it already. So it was good to hear it from someone finally. She was mur--" Her voice caught on the word, and she had to start again. "She was murdered in Ridge Point? Did they find her?"

"No, but we might know where she is." Cheryl needed Anne's help to find out the whole truth about what happened to Tanya.

"Why didn't the police come? Why would they send a psychic to tell me that my daughter is dead?" She looked from Cheryl to Adam for an answer.

"They are so busy right now." Cheryl recalled the chaos in the police station.

Anne blotted her eyes with a tissue. "I've seen the reports. It's just horrifying. Who would've thought that something like that would happen in these parts."

"Do you know anything about the man your daughter was seeing before she disappeared?" Cheryl asked.

"She never mentioned anyone." She held her finger up as if asking for a moment. "Wait a minute. She did mention a male friend once. When she talked about him, I noticed the way her voice changed. It always raised in pitch when she talked about a boy she liked when she was a teenager. I used to think it was so cute. When she got older, it became less cute and more worrying because of her taste in men. She liked older men, unsavory characters mostly. I didn't understand the draw. Maybe it was because she never really knew her father."

Cheryl nodded. "Did you ever meet him?"

"No. It was hard enough for me to get her to admit there was anyone. She was hardly talking to me then. That's why the police didn't take my report seriously at first. They said she probably ran off and didn't tell me." Tears welled up in Anne's eyes again. She wiped them away. "I knew something was wrong." Her voice hitched. "I just knew it. You think she was dating Mark?"

"We can't be sure. We're just asking questions right now. Did she tell you anything about this guy?" Adam asked.

"Nothing really."

"So you have no idea if she was with him the day she disappeared?" Adam was starting to sound like a police detective.

"No. How could I know? She was just a few hours away, but a lot of times, it felt like she lived halfway around the world." She began to cry again. "I'm sorry."

"Don't be. You've gone through a lot already. I hate to ask you this, but I need you to call the police in Ridge Point and tell them that you suspect that your daughter was killed. Tell them that you got an anonymous tip that she was drowned in the lake at the property on 4444 Pine Road. Demand that they search for her." Cheryl gave her instructions, slowly watching Anne's response.

"I thought you said you were working with the police?" She wiped her eyes with the balled-up tissue.

"I'm trying to, but they're not listening." Cheryl's voice tightened.

"So you lied to me?" Betrayal cut through her words.

Cheryl shook her head. She hadn't thought of it as a lie because she was trying to convince the police to do what was necessary to find Tanya's body. "No. I know where Tanya's body is because she showed me. She comes to me in visions. When we got here, Tanya was showing me how she died."

Anne stood and walked across the room to the wall opposite Cheryl. Cheryl knew she didn't have long before Anne would put them both out.

Tanya crossed the room too. She stood next to her mother, both of their backs faced Adam and Cheryl.

"She's here now. Can you feel her?" Cheryl decided that now was the time to be bold. If Anne had an open heart, she would be able to feel that her daughter was with them.

Tanya moved in closer to her mother, so close now that if she were alive, they would be brushing against each other.

Anne shivered and crossed her arms over her chest.

"That's her," Cheryl said. "What you just felt was her. She wants you to know that she loves you. You were the best mother. She knew you were only trying to protect her, but she needed to make her own mistakes."

Tanya began to emanate a bright white light that enveloped her mother.

Anne turned around slowly. A series of emotions from fear to comfort flashed across her face. "I can feel something."

"That's her," Adam said.

"She's standing next to you right now. She is the one who sent us here. Do you know what she wants?" She didn't wait for Anne to answer the question. "She wants you to get the Ridge Point police to search that lake because that's where she is. She's waiting to get justice. Her boyfriend betrayed her. He drowned her in that lake, and she wants her body found along with the evidence. That's what she's waiting for. That's what she needs to find peace."

"How do I know you're not just trying to manipulate me to get something?" Anne began to sob again. "I don't know what you want from me? I don't have any money. All I have is this house."

"We haven't asked you for anything," Adam said. "We aren't going to."

"We just want the police to believe us. We're trying to help your daughter. That's all we want." Cheryl said.

Anne sniffled. "What if I don't believe you?"

They were wearing out their welcome. Cheryl could see that. She stood up slowly, still feeling a bit wobbly. Adam took hold of her hand to steady her. "We'll get out of your hair." They started to the door. "You don't have to believe us. You just have to make the call."

They left her standing in the middle of the living room as they walked out the door down the porch steps.

"Do you think she'll do it?" Adam asked as they walked up the front walk to the car.

"She'll be on the phone before we even pull out of the driveway. I'm sure of it."

As they backed out of the short driveway, Cheryl could see her through the window, the phone pressed against her ear.

Chapter 12

They'd only gotten halfway back to Ridge Point when Adam's phone rang. "Hello?"

"Is this Adam Green?"

He recognized the voice right away. "Detective Haskell," Adam said, smirking at Cheryl.

"We just got an unexpected call back at the station. Tanya Garrett's mother wants us to search that lake for her body. She says she got an anonymous tip."

"Did she really? That's a coincidence." Adam winked at Cheryl.

"I was thinking the same thing. You wouldn't happen to be that anonymous tip, would you?"

Adam ignored his question. "Since the mother of the victim seems to have the same idea we do, maybe it's about time to search that lake." He raised an eyebrow at Cheryl, who sat in the passenger seat waiting for his answer.

"So now you have a victim's name. Where did you get that?" Detective Haskell asked.

"We have our sources," Adam said. "You didn't think we were going to stop our investigation just because you refused to help us, did you?"

"She also seems to think that her daughter's death is somehow connected to the Ridge Point serial killer,"

Detective Haskell said.

"She might be onto something," Cheryl couldn't help herself.

"Oh, I'm talking to both of you." He spoke slowly, the words curled around them. "I'm calling to give you a warning. Stay out of police business."

"Or?" Adam and Cheryl asked together.

He took longer to answer than he should've. The speakers buzzed from the bad connection. "Or I'll arrest you for interfering with a police investigation."

"Can you do that?" Cheryl asked.

He hung up before she'd even finished her question.

"He seems like he's in a bad mood," Cheryl remarked. "You'd think he'd be happy for the help. It's not like they were getting close to solving the case before we got here."

Adam chuckled. "You're terrible."

"Do you think they'll search the lake? I wish they would. Then we can put all of this behind us."

"We can't do that until Mark is in jail. I don't know about you, but I could never feel good about walking away knowing that he's still out there killing people." Adam kept glancing at Cheryl as he drove. They merged onto the highway and headed back toward Ridge Point. He reached into the cup holder and pulled out Tanya's necklace. The gold pendant gleamed in the sunlight. "We have to solve this for her and his next victim."

Cheryl reached out and took the chain from him. "I forgot all about this. Why didn't you show it to her mother?"

Adam had thought about telling Anne about the necklace but quickly realized that it would do more to make him look like the guilty party than prove that Tanya's ghost was telling them what had really happencd to her. "It didn't seem like a good idea."

Cheryl nodded. Her phone chirped in her purse. She pulled it out. "Day and Stephanie keep texting me." She turned her attention to her phone.

Traffic was light. Tired and anxious to find another motel to stay in, Adam sped along. Greenery streaked by them. At this rate, they'd get back to Ridge Point with plenty of time to find a new place to stay and get something to eat.

"I don't know why she's been blocking out Mark's face every time she shows me what happened to her." Cheryl put her phone down on her lap. "It must mean something, but what?"

She looked over at him, and seeing her face looking at his sent anger pulsing through him. It was like he was turning into someone else. His breathing sped up, and his heart raced. Dark emotions coursed through him, and he felt like he was losing control of himself. "Something's wrong." He barely managed to get the words out.

"What?"

"Nothing," he heard himself say. "Everything is exactly the way I want it to be." He yanked the steering wheel to the left, sending the car careening off the road.

**

Cheryl didn't know what happened. She'd been shocked by the bile in Adam's voice just before they crashed. Tires squealed. Horns blew. They veered off the road into a ditch at top speed. The airbags deployed with a whoosh, slamming into her. When everything stopped moving, she sat in the car listening, stunned. Something hissed. Someone yelled words she couldn't understand. When she realized what had happened, she turned her head and was glad to see Adam looked like he was okay too. He was trying to get out of the car, but the door was jammed. Cheryl pulled her door handle, and the door fell open, letting her tumble out into the grass.

"Are you okay?" A man came running down into the ditch at Cheryl, and her first instinct was to flinch. "What happened? Are you all right?" The man rushed over and put his hand on Cheryl's back.

Noticing Adam in the driver's seat, he ran over to the driver's side and tried to open the door. It was too late though; Adam had already hoisted himself up to crawl out the passenger side. "I called for an ambulance," the man said. He held his phone up to both of them as if looking at it would give some kind of proof.

"When you call 911, don't they usually make you stay on the phone until help arrives?" Cheryl asked.

"Oh, I didn't know that. I just told them where we were and hung up."

Just then, a blue and white ambulance skidded to a stop on the shoulder of the road. A slight woman in a black and blue uniform got out and ran down the side of the ditch toward them. "Is everyone all right?"

"I'm fine. I'm the one who called." The man motioned to Adam and Cheryl with a flourish. "They're the ones who need your help."

**

Adam told her that he lost control of the car, but in reality, he had lost control of his body. When they'd gone careening off the road, they'd narrowly missed hitting a tree. "I don't know what happened," he'd said when she asked him.

As the EMTs poked and prodded him, he kept an eye on Cheryl. She rubbed her neck as she talked. He hoped she wasn't hurt too badly. He wouldn't forgive himself if she was.

Suddenly, he realized that the EMT who had been examining him had stopped and was looking at him expectantly.

"I'm sorry, did you ask me something?" Adam asked the EMT.

He was a young man with a round, brown face and straight black hair that stuck up on his head in tiny spikes. His eyes seemed to rest back a little too far in the sockets. "I asked if you want to go to the hospital?" He blinked a few times. "You look like you're fine, but we can never be too sure. You might want to go in and get some tests. It's usually a good idea for insurance purposes."

"I'm fine. I think we can skip all the hospital bills." As he talked, he rotated his wrist around and checked his shoulders, ankles, and legs to be sure he really wasn't in any pain.

"Okay well, let me go find out what's going on with your passenger." The man trudged through the tall grass to Cheryl and the female EMT. Just then, the officer who had been sitting in his car on the shoulder of the road got out and walked down the hill toward the man who had made the call. They had a conversation. The witness was animated, his hands moving to and fro. Adam wondered what he was saying.

"Looks like you had a bit of an accident." The officer pointed at the car as he walked over to Adam.

"Unfortunately."

"What happened?" There was an edge to his voice that Adam didn't like.

"I don't know. I lost control of the car." Adam replayed the incident in his mind, looking for answers.

"You been drinking?" The police officer seemed to lean in a little bit as if trying to smell Adam's breath.

"No."

"On drugs?"

"No." Adam knew he probably had to ask, but the questions felt like accusations.

"Meth, cocaine, a little bit of weed, maybe?"

Adam didn't understand the need for this list. "I know what drugs are. The answer is still no."

"So if I go get a breathalyzer, you wouldn't have a problem with taking it." He pointed up the hill at his police cruiser.

"No, I wouldn't mind taking it because I haven't been drinking."

"So if we had some blood work done up, we wouldn't find any drugs?" The officer wouldn't look directly at him. Instead, his gaze bounced from the sky to the ground to Adam's car, sitting crumpled in the tall grass.

"Why are you treating me like a criminal? It was just an accident."

"It's not every day that someone runs off the highway for absolutely no reason. It's my job to make sure everything checks out. Who's the girl with you?" He nodded toward Cheryl.

"My business partner." Adam did his best to hide his annoyance.

"What kind of business?"

"Does it matter?"

"It might. We don't have business partners coming into this town and just running off the highway all the time. So, what kind of business are you in? Anything illegal?"

Adam shook his head. He didn't want to answer these questions. "This line of questioning is ridiculous."

"Maybe I have to bring you to the station."

"That won't accomplish much."

The EMT who had been talking to Adam strolled up to them. "We have to take your friend to the hospital. Do you want to ride along?"

Adam looked at the police officer. "I don't know. I might be getting arrested."

"You're not getting arrested, but you do need to come into the station."

Chapter 13

Cheryl couldn't believe it when she saw Adam walking away with the police officer. "Wait!" she called after them.

"We have to take you to the hospital, ma'am." The female EMT put her bony hand on Cheryl's shoulder, preventing her from getting up off the gurney.

"He should be going to the hospital with me." Cheryl pointed at Adam.

"We checked him out." The EMT let go of Cheryl and put her hand on her narrow hips. "He's fine. You don't have to worry. They just want to ask him some more questions about the accident."

"Let me go talk to him." She tore away from them and tried to run up the hill to Adam, but suddenly she felt woozy and had to stop. She leaned forward, putting her hands on her knees and her head down to steady herself.

"I'm fine. Go to the hospital. I'll be there soon," Adam called to her.

She watched as the police officer put him in the back of the squad car. This couldn't be good.

She felt the weight of a hand on her back. "Let's get you into the ambulance," the EMTs said.

Bile rose in her throat. "I think I'm going to be sick." She barely got the last word out before she opened her mouth and vomited in the long grass.

She didn't want to lie down in the ambulance; there was no reason for that. She felt bad but not bad enough to be taking this ride. All she could do was worry about the bill. She was sure this trip would bankrupt her.

"Is it normal for them to take somebody away for questioning after an accident? We weren't doing anything wrong." She swallowed, trying to keep the remaining contents of her stomach down.

"Sometimes, they do." The EMT motioned to the gurney. "I need you to lie down, and then I'm going to put this collar on you."

"But, I'm fine." Cheryl's neck did hurt, but she didn't want to admit it. She wanted to go to the police station with Adam.

"It's just a precaution."

Deciding to be more cooperative, she lay down and did what she was told. The collar felt like it was lifting her head clear up off her neck. It reminded her of the time when Mark tried to choke her. She remembered the panic that settled deep inside of her when she realized she could not get air and might never breathe again. Her breathing became fast and shallow as she replayed the incident in her mind. "Do I have to wear this?"

"Yes, if you have a neck injury, this will stop it from getting worse." The EMT looked at her with pity in her eyes. "Try to take some deep breaths." She inhaled and let the air out again.

Cheryl tried but couldn't imitate her. Instead, her breath became faster and shallower. "I think I'm having a panic attack." She panted.

"I can give you a sedative."

"How much is that?" She managed to ask. She gripped the side of the gurney as hard as she could.

"I don't know, but it will help you calm down." The EMT

got out a syringe. The ambulance had only just started the engine.

"No, thank you. I'll deal with it. I'm fine. I'm fine really," she said, eying the needle in her hand.

The ambulance lurched forward, and the siren blared.

"Are you sure? You don't have to suffer." She held the needle up as if seeing it would somehow change Cheryl's mind.

"I'm not suffering." Cheryl looked at the needle. "I'm totally fine."

As the ambulance sped along the highway, Cheryl closed her eyes and focused on taking even deep breaths. She'd gotten her panic attack under control; too bad she didn't have control over anything else right now. So many things were going wrong. "This trip was a bad idea," she said.

"Sorry you're having a bad day." The EMT looked genuinely empathetic. "I'm sure it'll get better once you're out of the hospital."

Cheryl thought about the car getting impounded and wondered how they would get around now. Their investigation kept getting more and more difficult. She was just about ready to give up when a drop of water landed in the center of her forehead.

Cheryl opened her eyes and saw Tanya Garrett floating above her. Her body seemingly part of the roof of the ambulance.

"Don't give up. You're so close," a voice in her head said.

**

"What's this all about?" Adam asked as the police car glided along the highway. It was strange to be in the back of the police cruiser. The lack of handles on the doors and the grate between him and the officers made him feel trapped. He knew that was the point but wondered what would happen if they were in a serious accident. Would he just be left there to die?

"We need to ask you a couple of questions at the station," the thin officer who was driving said. "It won't take long."

"You could've asked me back there. Why put me in the back of the police car?" The ambulance carrying Cheryl had left already. He pictured her alone in the back, worried about what was happening. He was worried too. "I should be with my girlfriend."

"I thought she was your business partner," the thin officer said.

"She's both."

He nodded and looked at Adam in the rearview mirror like he'd caught him in a lie.

"You'll be with her soon enough." The stocky officer in the passenger seat drew out his words.

Adam knew protesting was useless, so he sat back in the car and tried not to panic. He watched the back of the police officers' heads through the grate. They sat in quiet stillness as the world outside the car rushed by. Cold water seeped into Adam's shoes, pooling around his feet. It climbed up his ankles. He looked down to see the dark, murky water rising up his calves. He didn't panic. He knew what this meant. She was back. The seat shifted. He looked to his right to see her sitting calmly next to him. Her hair hung down in dark tendrils.

"You haven't stopped him yet?" She seemed to whisper directly into his brain.

I can hear you now, he thought. He didn't want to speak because he knew the officers might think he was crazy. He couldn't have that on top of driving the car off the road to

Lady in the Lake

deal with.

"He's killed someone else." The air seemed to contract, and she disappeared.

Adam exhaled. They were doing everything they could, but somehow it still wasn't enough.

The police sat him in a familiar room: beige walls, metal table, three chairs. They didn't have to tell him where to sit, he already knew. He took the chair facing the mirror. If anyone was watching, he wanted to give them a good view of his face, so they knew he was telling the truth. They left him in the room alone. He heard the keys outside jingle as they locked him in.

He watched the mirror on the wall opposite him and wondered if anyone was on the other side. Were they watching? What did they hope to see?

All of this was a waste of time. While they were getting ready to interrogate him about a completely inconsequential accident, someone else was dead. He couldn't tell them that though because he didn't know who, and he realized that talking about what little he knew could implicate him in the crime.

Adam was weighing his options when the door opened. The thin officer who had driven the car walked in. He was young, with a narrow face, acne-scarred cheeks, and a cocky attitude. "I have some questions for you. If your story checks out, you're free to go."

Adam wanted to ask what story he was talking about but thought it was best not to.

The questions he asked were all very un-extraordinary.

"How long are you expecting to stay in town?

"What happened exactly when the car went off the road?

"Were there any other vehicles on the road with you?

"Did you feel or see anything strange when the car went off the road?"

Adam answered each as honestly as he could. After going over the incident over and over again, his eyes felt heavy, and his thoughts began to slow. "Am I under arrest for something?"

"You look tired. How about some coffee?" The officer stood and left the room. Before the door clicked closed, someone caught it and pulled it open. The officer's stocky partner walked in, red-faced and sweating. He walked up to the table where Adam sat. His mouth twitched, and then pressing his palms flat on the table, he leaned across it. "You better be careful around here if you don't want to end up at the bottom of that lake too."

"Are you threatening me?" Adam furrowed his brow.

"I'm just explaining what could happen. How you choose to take that is up to you." He stood up straight and looked Adam in the eye, unblinking.

Before Adam could say anything else, his partner came back in carrying a steaming cup of coffee. He set it on the table in front of Adam along with a little creamer packet and some sugar packets.

"Your girlfriend's at County General," the slender cop said. "We'll take you over there."

Adam hoped he'd never get used to riding in the back of a police cruiser. Thankfully, the hospital wasn't far. He spent the whole time watching the back of the stocky officer's head. When they pulled up in front of the hospital, he got out to let Adam out of the car while the slender officer remained in the driver's seat.

When he opened the car door, he looked down at Adam with a sneer on his face. As Adam got out, he half expected the officer to slam the door on him, knocking him unconscious. Nothing of the sort happened, but the police officer whispered in his ear, "Stay away from Cheryl. That bitch will ruin you."

Taken aback, Adam asked, "What'd you say?"

The cop shook his head and pushed the door closed. "You heard me."

He got into the car, and they pulled away.

**

Cheryl lay on the gurney looking at the ceiling. She couldn't stop wondering about what was happening with Adam. Why had the police taken him away?

"We just need to get you a CT scan to make sure everything's okay with your neck," the young man in mint-green scrubs said to her. The gurney shifted as he unlocked the wheels. "It's time to go for a ride."

As he pushed her down the hall, Cheryl lay on her back, watching the white ceiling tiles and rectangular fluorescent lights pass by overhead.

She appreciated that he didn't bother making small talk. She needed time to reflect.

She thought about the SUV sitting in a ditch with their bags in it. Surely the car had been towed away by now. She wondered if it was drivable. She couldn't recall how badly it had been damaged.

The gurney stopped. "Wait here." The young man hurried through a door, leaving her parked in a room with a row of empty chairs against the wall next to her. She closed her eyes. Sleepiness started to overtake her, but she couldn't sleep now.

The door opened, and the young man came back into the room. "I'll be back to pick you up soon." The man hurried past her and out the door they'd come in.

The technician working the CT machine looked no older than 21. She explained what would happen in detail as if she were reading a script. Her blank gaze wandered around the room as she spoke. Her words droned into a mumble until she stopped midsentence. Cheryl looked at her expectantly, waiting for what she might say next, but she stood looking at the floor blankly as if she'd forgotten what she was doing.

"Are you okay?" Cheryl asked.

Then she grabbed hold of Cheryl's calf, hard. Her nails pressed into Cheryl's flesh. "Looks like you've had yourself an accident, huh? You weren't careful, were you? That was always your problem, too damned clumsy. You're lucky you've managed to survive as long as you have. You almost got yourself killed a few times when we were together. Bashing your face on things so many times, people started talking."

Cheryl sat up. "What did you say?"

The technician jumped back, her eyes wide with fright. "What's happening?" She looked around the room like she didn't know where she was. "Who are you?"

"Is this some kind of joke. It's not funny. It's not funny at all." Cheryl got off of the gurney that was a bit too high for her to reach the floor comfortably.

"I don't know what you're talking about," she said.

"I don't know what's going on here, but I'm leaving." Cheryl backed away from the technician.

"This scan is for your own safety. We just have to get a quick look at your neck, and then you can go home." The technician walked toward her, but her motions seemed unnatural. It was almost as if she were relearning how to use her body.

"Did you know Mark Hampton?" Cheryl asked. "Were you one of his girlfriends?"

"Who?" She grabbed hold of the wall, looking like she

Lady in the Lake

might topple over.

"Are you okay?" Cheryl asked.

The woman nodded. "I just need a--" Her head jerked up, and her whole demeanor changed. Her soft blue eyes hardened. The muscles around her jaw tensed.

The fear center in Cheryl's brain snapped into action, just as the technician lunged forward, grabbing hold of her wrist. "I should've killed you when I had the chance." Her voice slurred.

"Mark?" The word slid from her lips. She pulled away and ran for the door. The pain in her neck vanished as she sprinted up the hallway fueled by adrenaline. "Help!" she yelled.

"Get back here, you stupid whore!" The voice was different, but she knew those words.

Panic washed over her. "No!" What was happening? She wasn't sure, but she wasn't going to let Mark get to her again. The technician was still after her when Cheryl turned the corner, she fell to the floor.

"Are you okay? What's going on?" A man in navy blue scrubs asked her. He grabbed her by her elbow and helped her to her feet.

"She's after me!" Cheryl turned, pointing to the technician who had stopped running.

She stood in the middle of the hall, a blank expression on her face. She blinked a few times, then held her hand to her head and bent over. "What's going on? I don't feel good at all. I think something's wrong."

"She was chasing me, I swear. Don't trust her. She's not who you think she is." Cheryl knew she sounded like a crazy person, but she was used to sounding that way.

The man looked into her eyes and said, "It's going to be okay. I'll figure out what's going on. You stay right here." He let go of her arm and walked over to the technician.

"Samantha, are you okay?"

She shook her head. "No. I don't know what's going on. I think I blacked out."

Cheryl watched her looking for evidence of Mark but saw nothing now. Did that really happen, or did she imagine it?

A nurse in purple scrubs came around the corner. "Diane, Samantha's not feeling well. Could you take this patient back to get her CT scan?"

Diane looked startled at first but swiftly nodded her head. "What's wrong, Sam?"

Samantha shook her head. "I'm not sure."

"Rest up. I'll take care of this." Diane turned her attention back to Cheryl. "Let's get you your scan."

"I'm fine." Cheryl watched Samantha, who walked slowly up the hallway with the man. "I don't think I need one now." All she wanted to do was get out of the hospital.

"It won't take long," Diane reassured her as she led her back down the hall.

Chapter 14

Cheryl walked into the emergency room waiting area, pulling on her coat.

"I've been trying to get someone to give me some information about you for ages," Adam said as he joined her. "These people are so miserable, and they don't want to help with anything." He pointed at Cheryl and looked over to the woman behind the counter who was popping her gum. "See, she was here."

The woman rolled her eyes and shook her head before answering the ringing phone.

Cheryl zipped up her coat as they stepped out into the icy cold parking lot. "Mark was in there. He tried to kill me."

Adam turned and looked back at the hospital doors that still stood open. "We have to call the police." The police officer's threat was still fresh in his mind, but there was no one else to call.

"No. It wasn't like that. He was inside the body of the technician." She looked around like she was afraid he would jump out at her at any moment.

"Inside the body of the technician? What are you talking about?"

"I don't know." She took off across the parking lot.

"Where are you going?" Adam called after her. "We don't

have a car."

She stopped. An oncoming car beeped, and she spun around and stepped back up onto the sidewalk. "Is the car totaled?"

"Probably, but I don't know." He didn't even know where the car was.

"This is terrible. I'm so sorry. This all happened because of me." A tear slid down her cheek.

Adam put his arm around her shoulders. "I came with you because I wanted to. There was no way I'd let you go through all of this alone." He pulled her into him. It felt good to be with her again. "Tanya appeared to me in the police car. There's been another murder."

She pulled away from him and crossed her arms over her chest. Puffs of white condensation came from her mouth as she spoke. "I knew this would happen. Every second we waste gives him time to kill someone else."

He zipped up his coat, tucking his chin into the collar. "That's why we need to get moving."

"To where?" she asked. Her eyes were still glassy with tears.

He remembered the business card the tow truck driver gave him before he was shoved into the back of the police cruiser. Pulling the white card from his pocket, he read the name of the company. "I think it's here." He held the card out to her.

Cheryl sniffled. "Why is it so cold out here?"

"It's called winter. You used to live in these parts. You should know." He chuckled.

She grinned. "I'm so glad I moved." She shuffled back and forth in a kind of dance. "You call the tow truck people, and I'll try to get us a hotel room." She pulled her phone from her purse.

Lady in the Lake

"Sounds like a plan. I think we should go back inside to execute it." Adam gestured to the hospital doors.

**

Cheryl was supposed to be finding a hotel room for them to stay in that night, but she was so shaken by the events of the day that she could barely focus. The voice of the technician who was in the CT room played on a loop in her head. The way she had looked at Cheryl unnerved her. It was like she'd become Mark somehow, but that wasn't possible. Was it? If it was, could Mark become anyone in the waiting room with them now?

She eyed the people waiting in the emergency room. The man in the corner looking at his phone was tall and broad. He didn't look like he was sick at all. Could he be waiting for the perfect opportunity to attack her? She looked at Adam, who had his back turned to her as he talked on the phone. She could imagine Mark slipping inside of his body one day. She'd gone from not being able to find him to feeling like he's all around her.

"They have the car." Adam interrupted her thoughts. "We have to go fill out some paperwork. They say it's probably totaled, but they can't make the call. The insurance company has to do that. It's too late to go today. Let's find a hotel room, and we'll go over there first thing in the morning." He looked at her for a moment.

"Okay." She wiped a tear from her eye. "This is all too much."

"It's going to be okay. We'll get through it, and we'll turn Mark in. Our story has a happy ending." He smiled, but it seemed forced to her.

"I hope our story isn't over yet."

"It's far from over." He pulled up a ride-sharing app on his screen. "Did you find a place for us to stay? "

"Yeah." She took a few deep breaths trying to calm herself. She needed to stay sharp if she wanted to come out of this alive.

**

Adam didn't know what to think of Cheryl's story about what happened to her in the hospital. She'd been pretty shaken up by the accident, and he wondered how much it was affecting her perception. But how could she imagine that someone who worked at the hospital had threatened her life and chased her down the hallway? The cop had threatened him too. Or was he just imagining it?

Was all of this driving them both out of their minds? Since they'd arrived in Ridge Point, everything had been so full on and still there was no Mark. They didn't seem any closer to solving anything.

Cheryl slept heavily. He listened to her breathing as he lay in bed staring at the ceiling, waiting for Tanya to appear and tell him what to do next, but she didn't. She left him to worry through the night about how to make all of this turn out okay like he'd promised.

Chapter 15

They rented a little white sedan from the rental place near the hotel. The interior smelled vaguely of stale cigarettes, but they took it anyway. They were both too run down to complain.

Plympton's Body Shop was clear on the other side of town. A stray car door leaned against the telephone pole at the front of the property with a piece of weathered plywood mounted to it. The place's name was painted across the wood in dripping black letters.

Standing in the parking lot, Cheryl took a few deep breaths of the icy air before following Adam inside. Stained gray industrial carpet covered the floor of the wide-open space that greeted them. The fluorescent lights buzzed overhead. Two cheap, wood-veneer desks sat side by side in the center of the room. A round-faced woman sat at each desk. One had short brown hair streaked with gray and the other's hair was an unnatural shade of red. She perched her tortoiseshell-framed glasses on the end of her nose and said, "May I help you?" The question seemed more like an accusation than an offer of assistance.

Adam walked over to her briskly. "Yes, I called yesterday. You have my car."

She sifted through a stack of papers on her desk. "Adam Green?"

"That's right." Adam looked at the nameplate on her desk. "Susan." He flashed a smile at her, but Susan's mouth remained downturned.

"I have to see your driver's license." She handed him a clipboard. "And you need to fill this out."

Adam was struggling to get his driver's license out of the little slot in his wallet when Cheryl noticed a figure standing on the edge of her vision. She turned and looked, expecting to see someone else who worked there, but this was obviously not a worker. She knew because the side of the woman's face was crushed. Her ear was torn away, revealing gelatinous bits of gray brain matter. Cheryl swallowed hard. Fright bubbled up inside of her. She looked at the floor and then at Adam, trying the best she could to not let her gaze drift back over to the ghost, watching them with a worried look on her face. Cheryl closed her eyes, took a deep breath, and tried to relax. Every part of her tingled.

"Excuse me," she said. "Do you have a bathroom I can use?"

The woman at the desk next to Susan's, who had remained silent the whole time, twisted around and pointed across the room to a small hallway. "Sure. It's just back there."

"Thanks." Cheryl read the nameplate on her desk. "Deb."

Cheryl walked quickly across the room to the hallway. As she stepped into the dimly lit corridor, the woman appeared just in front of her. She jumped back, her hand on her chest. She looked behind her to make sure no one saw her. "Follow me," she whispered to the woman. She went into the bathroom and turned on the light.

"You can see me?" the ghost asked.

Cheryl stepped in close despite her grisly appearance. "Is there something you need from me?"

A tear slid down the ghost's cheek, and she wiped it away.

Lady in the Lake

"I can't believe you can see me."

"I can see you. I can't stay in here too long, so tell me what you need. I'm not going to make any promises, but I'll see what I can do to help you with any unfinished business." She wanted to feel like she could do something useful for someone while she was in this town.

She stepped closer to Cheryl and pushed her straight brown hair back behind her ear. A clump of soil fell to the yellow tile floor with a thud. She opened her mouth to speak again, and even more, soil cascaded out of her mouth to the ground. She coughed. "My head hurts." She held her hand up to cover the gooey part on her head. "It hurts so much."

"What do you need me to do? Why are you here?" Cheryl glanced at the door and wondered if anyone could hear her talking to herself. "What's your name?"

"Ashley," she croaked.

Cheryl sighed, relieved that she answered her so easily. "Good. Ashley, what's your last name?"

"Winter."

Why couldn't they all be this easy? "What do you need from me?"

She hacked again this time, bending over.

Cheryl closed her eyes for a moment. "Ashley, what do you want from me?"

"Find him. He has to pay!" Ashley's eyes met Cheryl's. Anger shot from them. "You can't let him kill anymore."

Cheryl swallowed hard. "Who?" She didn't have to ask. She knew.

"Don't pretend with me." Her voice deepened, and Cheryl felt afraid.

"Where did he bury you? I need evidence to get the police to listen to me."

"This is beyond what the police can handle. You have to

113

do it yourself." Ashley tilted her head, and pink goo dripped from her wound.

Cheryl's stomach turned. She looked at the floor and focused on not vomiting. "Where did he bury you?"

Ashely sneered. "Right under their noses. He's been doing it all right under their noses. It's more fun that way." Ashely vanished, leaving the rich smell of soil behind.

**

Cheryl meandered out of the bathroom with a vague look of confusion on her face. Adam sat in a folding chair against the wall, filling out paperwork. She sat down next to him. "Are you okay?" he asked.

She leaned in, whispering in his ear. "I just saw another ghost in the bathroom. She told me her name. She says Mark killed her too."

"Is she the latest victim in the news?"

"I don't know. She didn't say." She looked at him with wide eyes.

"What's her name?" He knew they needed as much information as possible.

"Ashley Winter. She told me that he's doing all of this right under everyone's noses."

Adam rubbed the back of his neck. "What does that mean?"

"I don't know. She disappeared before I could ask her any more questions." Cheryl glanced over at the hallway that led to the bathroom. "Hopefully, she'll show up again so I can get more information."

Susan looked up from her desk. "I'm sorry, but I couldn't help but overhear."

Adam and Cheryl exchanged worried glances.

Lady in the Lake

"We were just talking about a screenplay we're writing." Adam blurted out.

Cheryl gave him a sideways glance.

The woman lifted an eyebrow at him. "So, you're writers?"

"Yeah. We came here to do research." Cheryl fell in with the lie easily. "That case going on around here is fascinating. It makes good material."

"You mean the Ridge Point Killer?" Susan asked.

"Yeah." Cheryl was a bit too enthusiastic.

"It's been terrifying. By the time I get off from work, it's already dark, and I'm usually the only person closing up. I'm scared to go out to my car by myself. I call my husband and talk to him the whole way out to my car just so he knows I got there safely. He thinks I'm a bit too dramatic. The likelihood of anything happening to me is low really, but you never know." She thought for a moment. "How can someone just run around killing people like that. I don't understand it."

"It's not meant for you to understand, honey." Deb finally spoke. "If you understood anything about it, he'd be easier to catch. If it was understandable, it wouldn't have been going on for this long." She sniffed and pulled a tissue out of her pocket to dab her nose. "I think it's terrible people like you coming into town treating people dying like some sort of sideshow attraction. These are people's lives. We're terrified."

"It's not like that at all," Cheryl said.

"It's research, and we think we might be able to help them solve the case." Adam hated the idea of them thinking that he was exploiting the situation in any way.

"How exactly?" Susan asked.

"The cops haven't been able to figure it out yet. I hear the FBI is involved too." Deb looked at them expectantly.

"I'm not sure," Adam confessed.

"We've gotten some insider information," Cheryl said

more than she should've.

"Really?" Deb said. "You're not willing to share it, are you?"

"Sorry. We're not allowed to share that with anyone yet," Cheryl said.

"Too bad," Susan said. "Well, if you really can help them, I hope you do soon. We'll all be safer without him out there."

**

The frozen mud was hard beneath their feet as they walked through the field littered with wrecked cars. Adam's car sat at the edge of the lot. The entire front was smashed in like an accordion. The deflated airbags hung from the steering column and the dashboard. Looking at the wreck gave Cheryl a sinking feeling. She couldn't believe she had been in the car when it had happened.

"I had no idea it was this bad," Cheryl said to Adam. She reached out and took hold of his arm as they walked up to the car.

"It's pretty bad. Definitely totaled," Adam said. He had a wistful look in his eyes that made her wonder what he was thinking.

"I guess it's time to get a new car."

"I guess so. I always said I was going to drive this one into the ground. I certainly did that." He laughs dryly.

He opened the back and pulled out their bags. He unzipped his black duffel bag and opened the rear doors of the car.

"Make sure you get all your belongings out." Susan stood a few feet away with her arms crossed. She wore a black knitted turtleneck and hadn't bothered to put on her coat to come outside. "It's probably going to the scrapyard from here."

"Did you leave anything in the front seat?" Adam asked Cheryl. He opened the passenger door.

She shrugged. "I don't think so." She saw Ashley Winter again out of the corner of her eye. When she turned her head to look, she was standing just beyond the field in the snow. She beckoned for Cheryl with her hand. "What's over there?" Cheryl asked Susan, pointing toward where the ghost stood.

Susan squinted against the sun. "Nothing but a whole lot of snow." She shivered. "I'm going to go back inside. When you're done come back in and let me know before you go."

"Sounds good," Adam said.

She turned and carefully navigated the few yards of frozen ground to get the side door of the building. The door banged closed when she went inside.

Adam had climbed into the car now. Leaning over the front seat, he cleared out the glove box. "It's cold out here. You can go inside too if you want."

"Sure," Cheryl said as she walked in the opposite direction of the building past the car into the snow, drawn to Ashley, who stood in the distance waiting for her. The snow crunched beneath her feet. She wished she had boots but couldn't be concerned with getting her socks wet. She had to see what this ghost was trying to show her, so she continued onward. Her feet nearly slipped out from under her as she went up the slight rise of the incline that Ashley stood on. When she finally got to the spot, she found an exposed patch of dark ground with a light dusting of snow over it.

"He buried me here before the freeze." Her voice seemed to echo in Cheryl's head. Ashley reached out to Cheryl, and as her fingertips passed through her, Cheryl shivered and fell to the ground.

Hands gripped Cheryl's throat, cutting off the air. She

tried to inhale, but nothing would come in. She reached up, scratching at the flesh of the person above her. "I'll show you!" he growled. "You think you can talk to me like that. You're just like my wife." Her head hit the ground hard.

When she opened her eyes, Adam was standing over her. "What happened?" He squatted down next to her.

"He buried her here." Cheryl's throat still ached. She tried to take in a deep breath and wheezed and coughed.

"Who?"

"Ashley, the ghost I saw in the bathroom. She's here."

"Come on. Let's get you out of the snow." He helped her to her feet.

"She showed me what happened." The tears began to well up as emotions fluttered over her. "It was Mark."

"We have to tell the police there's another body." Adam pulled his phone from his pocket to call Detective Haskell.

Chapter 16

Cheryl leaned heavily on Adam's shoulder as he walked her down the hill through the snow. "We have to call the police." Seeing the place where the body was buried made Tanya's message about another murder painfully real.

"I don't know if that's a good idea." Her voice was weak, but he knew she would get stronger soon enough.

"We need help. I know the police aren't exactly willing to listen to us, but they'll need to know where the body is." He didn't look forward to trying to convince Detective Haskell to come out and take a look at what they'd found. "We can't stop Mark alone."

"Ashley told me that I have to."

He tilted his head at her. "What do you mean?"

"I don't know," she said.

He thought about putting her into the car to rest for a moment, but it was so cold. "Why don't you go inside and warm up while I finish cleaning out the car?"

"That's a good idea." She walked across the parking lot like every step took a great deal of thought.

The warehouse door squealed as Adam pushed it open. They stepped into the inviting warmth. Susan and Deb looked up from their desks at the same time.

"Do you mind if she sits inside while I finish cleaning out the car?" Adam stood with his arms still around her back in the doorway.

"You don't look good." Susan stood and hurried over to them.

"I'll be fine. I'm just starting to feel a bit woozy, that's all," Cheryl said weakly.

"Sit down over there." Susan took Cheryl by the forearm and led her to the folding chairs against the wall. "Have a seat and rest up. You look like you might pass out."

"Thank you," Cheryl and Adam said simultaneously.

"Do you want some coffee or tea?" Deb walked over to the round table where the single-cup coffee maker sat next to a brown wicker basket full of pods. She picked up a white Styrofoam cup. "A hot drink will warm you up."

"Coffee would be great." Cheryl's shoulders hunched like she was carrying the weight of the world.

Adam watched her as Deb made her a cup of coffee. He had so many questions, but he couldn't ask them here. "You'll be all right waiting here?"

She looked up at him, and he could see the fear in her dark eyes, but he knew she'd be okay.

"She'll be fine," Susan said.

Adam walked back through the lot to his totaled car. The front of the car was so smashed that he found it hard to believe they'd escaped the accident without any injuries. He opened the back door. Papers and trash were strewn around on the back seat. Most of what was in the car was garbage, but he had to be sure to go through everything because once it was gone, it was gone. The frigid air pushed in on him, tightening the muscles in his low back as he looked through papers, many of them discarded receipts. He wondered which ones he needed to keep for his taxes. He wished he had been more organized.

Reaching under the seat, he pulled out a lightweight

paperback, <u>A Book For New Visionaries</u>. A blonde with feathered hair looked out from the cover. If he was supposed to be a visionary, how come he hadn't seen whatever Cheryl had seen? Why was only one ghost coming to him? He flipped through the pages of the book casually before putting it into his duffel bag.

He took Tanya's necklace from the cup holder, holding it up by the delicate gold chain. He tried to imagine it hanging around her neck. Why had she chosen to show herself to him? Did he have something special to offer? Could he help her in a way that no one else could?

Standing in the parking lot, he stretched his arms over his head and looked out into the field where he had found Cheryl passed out. He wondered if he could make himself see whatever it was she had seen. Leaving his duffel bag on the back seat and the car door wide open, he walked over the frozen ground past the mangled corpses of vehicles to the footprints she'd left in the snow. He did his best to take a deep breath, but his lungs didn't want to accept too much of the icy air. He stepped forward in the snow, returning to the place where he'd found Cheryl.

The spot wasn't far from the parking lot. The snow crunched beneath his feet as he walked. When he got there, he noticed the ground had been disturbed. He squatted at the spot, and taking the glove from his hand, reached out his bare hand to touch the dirt. Other than cold and dirt and snow, he felt nothing. Frustrated, he yanked the glove from his pocket and put it back on. "Who are you? What happened here?" he asked the air. He stood. Beyond the field, he could see a chicken-wire fence constructed with thick, uneven wooden poles. A field of undisturbed snow reflected the sunlight beyond the fence. "You can tell me. I'm waiting." He listened and heard nothing, not even the whisper of a breeze.

Disappointed that the ghosts were hiding from him, Adam walked back through the field to the car. As he approached it, he saw something dark moving around in the back seat.

"Hey!" He tried his best to run on the slippery ground. "Get out of my car!"

When he reached the car, he realized it wasn't a thief in his backseat. It was Tanya. Water ran down her body like she was standing under a waterfall. Adam walked right up to her. This time there was no fear inside of him.

She held a finger up to her lips as if to shush him. Then she extended that same finger straight ahead of her. He followed the line of her finger to the building. Then he looked back at her.

"He brought me there once." Her voice creaked like a squeaky door.

Adam looked back at the building. "You've been here before with Mark?"

Then she twisted around and pointed out into the field where Adam had just come from. "He's been here again."

Then she vanished.

**

Cheryl's toes tingled as the feeling came back into her feet. They were still cold and wet, but at least the building was warm. She wrapped her fingers around the warm Styrofoam cup and breathed in the rich aroma of the coffee.

"This must be a real change from Florida," Susan said.

"Yeah," Cheryl's teeth still chattered. "I'm from here originally though."

"Really?" Susan raised a thin, overly arched eyebrow. "Whereabouts?"

"Right here in Ridge Point."

Lady in the Lake

"I bet you can't wait to get back to the warm weather." Deb picked up the yellow mug on her desk and took a sip of coffee. "Do you like your coffee? It's my favorite."

Cheryl had just been using the Styrofoam cup to warm her hands and hadn't even tasted the coffee yet. She took the slip, and the warm liquid filled her mouth. It was so good to get something hot in her belly. "It's perfect."

The front door swung open, bringing in a blast of cold air. A tall, thin man walked inside. His coveralls were grimy gray with a black and white nametag. He wore an old baseball cap on his head. The bill was deeply creased from years and years of wear. Tufts of mousy brown hair stuck out from underneath. He walked over to Deb's desk and dropped a set of keys on it.

"This is my last one for the day." He looked through some papers on the clipboard he had before removing them and giving them to Deb. "The car's already in the lot."

"That's fine, Gary." Deb immediately started flipping through the paperwork. "It's not like you to take off early. What's going on?"

"Nothing serious. I have to go to the dentist."

Deb nodded her head as she continued to look through the paperwork. It was obvious that she wasn't really listening.

Gary scanned the office, his eyes sweeping across Cheryl but completely ignoring her presence. Cheryl was glad to be ignored. He reminded her of Mark. He had the same unjustified confidence. She could imagine Mark working in a place just like this. He went to the door and lifted the brim of his cap just a bit with his right hand before saying, "I'll see y'all later."

As soon as the door closed, Cheryl exhaled. He wasn't Mark. Of course, he wasn't, but she wondered if he could've had some connection to this place. "You wouldn't happen to know someone named Mark Hampton, would you?"

"You know Mark?" Susan looked up from the paperwork on the desk.

Cheryl's heart began to thump in her chest. Maybe this was why the accident happened in the first place. "Kind of." She didn't want to tell them that she had been married to him for years. She thought that might affect what they would say.

"He used to work here. He was a piece of work that one." Deb shook her head. "He didn't last long."

Cheryl's heart pounded. "How long ago was that?"

"I don't know," Deb said. "A year and a half ago, maybe. He only managed to stick around for a month."

"It's such a shame about what happened. I can't say that I was surprised though," Susan added.

"What happened?" Cheryl asked.

Deb and Susan exchanged knowing looks.

"I don't want to be the bearer of bad news, but he died about a year ago--crashed his truck. They brought it in here, and it was smashed up real bad. I think it might've been one of the worst wrecks I've ever seen."

All the air rushed out of Cheryl's lungs. She reached down to put her cup of coffee on the floor before putting her head between her knees.

"Are you okay, honey?" Susan rushed over to her.

"I just feel a bit faint." She'd spent so much time running from Mark that she had never even considered that he might have died.

"You were close to him when you lived here?" Deb asked.

"I used to be married to him." Cheryl blurted out without thinking. She looked up and saw that both Susan and Deb were standing in front of her now, looking down at her with pity in their eyes.

"You poor woman. I can't even imagine how terrible that

must've been. I used to wonder how that poor girl stayed with him." Deb sat in the chair next to Cheryl.

"Monica has fallen to pieces since the accident." Susan leaned forward as if sharing a secret. "He treated her something terrible. She should've been dancing in the streets when she found out he was dead."

"You're terrible," Deb said, but her smile said something completely different.

Cheryl didn't know what to think. If Mark had been dead all this time, who were they looking for? Who was killing these women? Had Tanya sent them on a wild goose chase? Emotions cascaded through her. Without warning, she began to cry. The tears streamed from her eyes so quickly that it blurred her vision. "I'm sorry." Embarrassed, she covered her face with her hands.

"You poor dear." Susan rested a reassuring hand on her back. "You must've suffered so much."

"He was a mean drunk." Cheryl couldn't explain why sadness was mixed in with all these emotions she was feeling. Shouldn't she have been happy he was gone? Didn't his death put the whole reason they were there to rest? "I'd hate to think that some other woman had to suffer through what I did with him."

"Maybe he changed, and Monica's experience with him was completely different," she said it to be nice, but Cheryl didn't feel like it was true. She wasn't sure why she'd suddenly decided she needed to be nice about him at all.

"It wasn't." Susan shook her head knowingly. "I saw him slap her in the produce department in Walmart."

"Do you know what happened?" Cheryl asked. She still couldn't believe it. "The accident. How did it happen?"

Susan looked up at Deb as if asking her to answer the question. "He hit a tree. He must've been going full speed because the truck was so mangled."

"Drunk?" Cheryl asked. She didn't need to. He was always drunk.

"I assume so, but I don't know for sure. You'd have to ask the cops about that."

"What about Monica? Is she still around? I'd like to talk to her." She wasn't sure what she'd talk to Monica about, but maybe she knew something about Tanya.

"Yep." Deb was fast to answer. "She waits tables at the diner in downtown Ridge Point. She's a skinny little thing with black hair with hot pink streaks and a nose ring. What's her last name?"

"Williamson," Susan answered.

Cheryl nodded. Her thoughts raced. If Mark was dead, that meant that he wasn't the serial killer. She was still trying to adjust to the idea when Adam burst through the door.

Chapter 17

Adam opened the door a little more aggressively than he intended, making it slap against the opposite wall. He stepped in from the cold, carrying his duffel bag and wheeling Cheryl's small suitcase behind him. He was shaken from what Tanya had told him but decided to cover it up with a sense of false urgency. "Thanks so much for letting her sit inside." He hadn't even really looked around the room before he started talking. When he did, he saw Susan sitting on the couch next to Cheryl, whose head was down on her knees. Deb stood near them, looking down worriedly with her arms crossed over her chest.

"What happened?" He rushed over to Cheryl.

He placed his hand on Cheryl's shoulder, and she looked up at him with glassy eyes. "Mark's dead."

"That can't be right." He looked behind him at the building door. Why would Tanya have told him what she did if Mark was already dead?

"He is. He definitely is," Susan said.

The news was so hard to process. They had come here with the intention of catching a dead man. What did Tanya want if her killer was already dead? How could they bring her justice? Despite the news, he still wanted to leave. "We should get going."

Deb and Susan jumped into professional mode. "You cleaned out the vehicle?" Susan asked. She went over to her desk and picked up a piece of paper. "I need you to initial and sign this saying that there are no personal items left in the car." She motioned for Adam to come over to her.

"How did you find out Mark was dead?" he asked as he signed.

"We got his truck after the accident," Deb said.

Adam nodded the whole time, but the information wasn't quite registering. Something wasn't right. "When was this?"

"About a year ago," Susan said.

He gave a sharp nod, but he still couldn't believe it. "Is that all that you need from me?" He motioned to the paper on Susan's desk.

"Yep." Susan pushed her glasses up with her index finger.

"Okay. Thanks for your help. We should get going." He gestured to Cheryl, who stood up slowly.

"Thank you for the coffee." She waved at them before following him out the door.

Adam called the police as they drove away.

"Detective Haskell?"

"Yes." The detective was hesitant.

"This is Adam Green. We met earlier."

"Oh yeah, the paranormal investigator." His words carried a mocking tone. "Let me guess. You have another tip for me."

At that moment, Adam questioned what he was doing. He wondered if he should even bother telling the detective what he knew. He looked over at Cheryl, who was staring silently out the window.

"Actually, I do." He waited for a moment expecting the detective to burst out laughing. When he didn't, Adam continued. "I was just over at Plympton's Body Shop and noticed something strange just east of their lot. There is a piece of ground that looks like it was dug up before the freeze last night. I'm guessing there is a body buried there. It's probably the work of your serial killer."

"And what makes you guess that?" Detective Haskell asked. Adam could hear the busy rush of the police station in the background. He wondered how long the lines were in the lobby and how many tips they'd received that day. He knew all of these facts probably affected whether or not Detective Haskell would follow up.

"There is a woman who's missing, Ashley Winter."

Detective Haskell began to speak before Adam finished what he was saying. "Who told you about Ashley Winter?"

"It doesn't matter." Adam didn't bother to give him any details. He didn't tell him where to find the spot. He didn't give them the address for Plympton Body Shop. He figured it wasn't worth wasting his time. The police obviously weren't going to act on his tip. Why would they? They thought of him and Cheryl as two crazy kooks who came to town because of the Ridge Point Murders. They definitely weren't worth listening to. He hung up without even saying goodbye.

"They're not going to check it out." She sounded defeated.

"Probably not." They really were in this all alone.

They drove in silence, letting the whole situation sink in.

Adam broke the silence. "I saw Tanya in the parking lot. She told me Mark had been there." He'd thought she'd meant more recently. He assumed she was telling him that Mark had killed the person buried beneath the frozen ground in that field. Now he knew that all his assumptions were wrong.

"Yeah, to work, apparently." She spoke softly.

"How are you doing with the news?" He realized he was only thinking about how Mark's death would affect what they were doing in Ridge Point. He hadn't even considered how it might make Cheryl feel.

"It's weird. Even though I've been running from him all this time, I assumed eventually I'd have my moment to confront him and show him that I was okay despite everything he did to try to destroy me." She pursed her lips and looked at the ground. "The truth is I'm getting better, but I'm still not okay, you know?"

"I know."

She looked at him. "The worst part is now that he's gone, there is the danger that he'll show up in my life one day. Distance doesn't protect me anymore. He might come looking for me."

He'd considered that too. "Maybe that's why Tanya implied that you were in danger." His memory flashed back to that moment and the dread he felt.

"Maybe." She leaned back in the seat and closed her eyes. "Worrying about it now won't help. We still need to get the police to find Tanya's body."

"And we need to figure out who killed her." Adam just wanted to sleep. They'd been through so much, and the day wasn't close to being over.

**

Cheryl sat in the booth, looking around the restaurant while Adam looked at the menu.

"So you know what you're going to eat?" he asked her.

She looked down at the laminated menu and chose the first thing she saw. "I'm just going to have a grilled cheese."

She watched a waif-like waitress trudge around the restaurant. "I bet that's her." Cheryl nodded in her direction.

Adam turned around to get a good look at her.

She was small but drove her feet into the ground like

jackhammers as she walked. Cheryl wondered how she didn't hurt herself doing all that stomping. Eventually, she made her way over to their table.

"What can I get you folks?" Her mouth formed a smile, but her gold-flecked eyes told a different story.

They ordered their food, and just before their waitress turned to walk away, Cheryl asked, "Are you Monica Williamson?"

"That's right." She lifted her head in acknowledgment of her name.

"Do you have a minute?" Cheryl had so many questions for her.

Monica narrowed her eyes at them. "Who are you?"

"My name is Cheryl and this is my partner Adam. We're here looking into a case."

"What are you, cops?" She eyed them suspiciously. "I can't help you with any case."

"You don't even know what it's about yet." Her refusal surprised Cheryl.

"It doesn't matter. I can't help you." She turned to walk away again.

"Monica, I'm Mark's wife."

She spun around to face them. All the blood drained from her face.

"I just want to know what was going on with him before he died." Cheryl continued.

Monica's knees buckled, and Cheryl thought for a moment that she might fall down, but she caught herself. "I can't talk about that. Not now." Her eyes swept around the dining room. Then she turned on her heels and walked straight back into the kitchen.

Monica didn't come back out of the kitchen for what felt like ages. Instead, a chubby blonde served her tables. As the blonde set the grilled cheese in front of her, Cheryl asked, "Where's Monica?"

"She's not feeling very good, but I can help you with anything you need. Is there anything else you want?" She stood in front of them with one hip jutted out to the side, waiting for an answer.

"Did Monica go home?" Adam asked.

The waitress shook her head. "Not yet, but I told her she should."

Monica tramped out of the kitchen and made a beeline for their table. Her eyes were red from crying. "Okay. I'm ready to talk." She sounded resigned.

"These people upset you?" The blonde scowled at them.

"It's fine. They just had some questions about Mark. I'm going to talk to them for a few minutes." Monica pulled nervously at the short, red apron wrapped around her hips.

"If they give you any trouble, let me know. I'll be checking on you." The blonde spoke firmly, making sure to give them a dirty look before leaving to take another table's order.

Cheryl scooted over so Monica could sit down next to her. The vinyl-covered cushions creaked. When she had settled, Cheryl wasted no time. "Look. I know it was terrible. He tried to kill me, and that's why I left."

"He was pretty awful. That was Mark. He threatened my life almost every day. There were more than a few times when I thought he would kill me." She sniffled and wiped her nose with her hand. Thin strands of hair fell down around her eyes.

"You're lucky he didn't. Guess we're both lucky because I think he might've killed someone else."

"I wouldn't be surprised." Monica looked at the table.

"Do you know Tanya Garrett?" Adam asked.

Monica shook her head.

"I think he murdered her not long before he died. Did you

notice anything suspicious going on before the accident?"

She thought for a moment. "Not any more than usual." She scanned the restaurant, then lowered her voice. "This will probably sound crazy, but he's still around. I can feel him watching me." Fear played across her face.

A chill shot through Cheryl.

"What do you mean?" Adam asked.

"Once he told me that I was going to be afraid of all the power he'd have. Soon he wouldn't even have to worry about the cops." She crossed her thin arms over her chest. "He was drunk, so I didn't think it meant anything. He used to say a lot of things when he was drunk, but..." Her voice hitched. She looked at the swinging door to the kitchen nervously.

"But what?" Cheryl leaned in a little closer.

She shrugged. "I think he figured something out. I found all these weird books after he died."

"What kind of books?" Adam leaned forward in his chair.

"I don't know how to explain them. They were like spell books you see in movies or something. I looked through a few of them, but they creeped me out." She gave an exaggerated shiver. "So, I threw them away."

"Do you remember anything specific about the books?" Cheryl had such high hopes for meeting Monica. She needed to pry as much information from her as possible.

She shook her head. "Just that they were old and they had what looked like recipes, but when I read them, they called for strange ingredients like rusty nails and powdered human bones." She opened her eyes wide.

"What do you think he was trying to do?" Cheryl asked.

"There's no trying about it. He did it. I know because he comes here sometimes and threatens me, but he's different every time." She looked around the restaurant. "He could be here now. He could be overhearing this whole conversation."

"I don't understand," Adam said. "He's dead, but you're saying he comes here to harass you sometimes? As a ghost?"

Monica shook her head. "No. As a person who's alive. As someone else. He might be a homeless guy one day or the woman who comes in every Tuesday afternoon for coffee and a piece of pie another day."

"You think he's possessing these people?" This wouldn't be the first time Cheryl heard about such a thing, but she wouldn't think that Mark could have such an ability.

"Yeah." Monica didn't hesitate.

"How do you know?" Adam asked.

"The things those people say to me are things only Mark would say. It's like he's crawled inside them. I can see him in their eyes before they even open their mouths. He's messing with me. Maybe he's trying to drive me crazy." Monica sighed. "He's succeeding."

"He's after me too. He knows I'm here." Suddenly everything started to come together for Cheryl. The bum in the restaurant. The man outside the motel. The CT scan technician. Of course, they were all Mark.

Monica leaned back in her seat. "I knew I wasn't crazy. He's still here." Fresh tears flowed down her cheeks. She wiped them away with the napkin. "I don't think him smashing into that tree was an accident."

"Do you think someone murdered him?" Adam asked.

Monica shook her head. "I think he did it on purpose because he'd found a way to stick around even after he was dead."

Cheryl thought she knew the kind of evil Mark was capable of but never imagined this. "Do you have any proof that he was planning something like this?"

She shook her head. "I don't have any of his stuff. I threw it all away. Sold what I could, of course." She bit her lip and looked down at the table like she was trying to think of something. "There are these people he used to hang out with, this old guy and his wife. They were kind of creepy. I was in the car when he had to stop by there and pick up something once. I don't know the exact address, but I can tell you where they live."

"A little yellow farmhouse by a lake," Cheryl said.

Monica's mouth hung open in disbelief. "How do you know?"

"We've already been there." Cheryl looked at Adam. "And it looks like we're going back."

Chapter 18

The sun sank on the horizon as they made their way up the bumpy single lane road. Adam focused on the drive, but so many questions swirled around in his mind. What were they going to say to the people that lived inside the house? How could they stop a ghost who seemed bent on causing death and destruction? Would they even be able to? He knew what he'd seen in the house in his vision and was terrified that going there again was walking Cheryl right into a trap. He would have to be vigilant to keep her safe.

Cheryl pulled at a strand of her hair and looked out the window. Occasionally, she'd break the silence with a statement. "He was worse than I even thought." She turned and looked at Adam, who kept his eyes trained ahead. "There really was a part of me that thought all of this was a mistake. Maybe Mark wasn't a killer, and Tanya showed him to me because she knew feeling that I was responsible would drive me into action. When I found out he died, I experienced so many emotions--shock, grief, disappointment but also relief. Which is weird, you know? I thought, 'Great. He isn't the serial killer after all,' but now this. What if he's doing what Monica thinks?" She looked out the window at the passing trees. "If all this is true, then that means I'm an even worse judge of character than I thought. He's bad. He's terrible. I knew that before, but this is a kind of evil I never even thought was possible. How could I have fallen in love with him? I feel like such an idiot."

"He tricked you. He tricked everyone he knew. You can't blame yourself." Adam glanced over at her and could see her jaw moving ever so slightly. He knew she was chewing on the inside of her cheek, something she always did when she was nervous. "You're going to be okay."

"You can't promise that." She looked at him with glassy eyes.

"You're right, but I can try my best to make sure it's true." He knew she still didn't realize he'd walk through fire for her.

She nodded ever so slightly. "Rationally," she was looking in his direction, but her eyes seemed to be focused on something in the distance, "I know none of this is my fault, but I still feel so ashamed. Yes, I misjudged Mark from the beginning. I knew that already, but to know that I'd misjudged so badly makes me doubt the other decisions I've made in my life."

"If anyone should be ashamed, he should be, but he isn't." If Mark weren't already dead, Adam swore he'd kill him himself.

He drove their rental around the bend and past the lake to the house. The lake was frozen now, and a layer of snow perched on each tree branch. He pulled into the freshly-shoveled driveway behind the black sedan already parked there. "We asked her before, and she denied everything. How are we going to get her to talk now?" He wondered aloud.

Cheryl bit her lip. "I'm not sure. I just want to come straight out and ask if she knows Mark. She probably won't admit it."

"She already denied knowing him once." Adam felt like they were walking around in circles. They kept seeming to get closer to the truth and somehow further away too.

"Well, it's time to find out." She opened the door.

They got out of the car. They could see someone inside through the front window. "Looks like they're home," Adam said.

The door swung open, and an older man stood in the entranceway. Puffs of gray hair stuck out each side of his head, and the top was bald. He smiled widely at them as they approached. His face was round and jolly. "Good evening." He enunciated his words carefully. "My wife told me you'd stopped by the other day. I've been wondering when you would return."

"I'm glad you've been expecting us." Adam did his best to play it cool even though he felt unnerved. "Would you be willing to answer a few questions?"

"Whatever for? Are you associated with the police or something?" The man smiled gleefully as he asked the question.

"Are you expecting to be questioned by the police?" Adam asked.

"Maybe we should start with introductions." The man's gaze shifted to Cheryl. "I'm Gene, and you met my wife, Patsy, before. You must be Cheryl." He nodded in Cheryl's direction. "And you are?"

"Adam. Adam Green." Adam took a step to the side, so he was directly in front of Cheryl because something about the way Gene looked at her made him feel uneasy. "Have you and Cheryl met before?"

"No. I haven't had the pleasure." Gene shifted his weight to peer around Adam and get a look at Cheryl.

"Dinner is ready." A woman's voice who Adam could only assume was Patsy called from somewhere inside the house.

Gene looked over his shoulder and then at Cheryl again.

Lady in the Lake

"Patsy's made supper early. Maybe you'd like to come and join us. We have plenty of food."

Adam looked back at Cheryl. He was just about to say no when Cheryl quickly answered for them.

"Thanks, but we ate a late lunch. We would love to come in for a moment though. If you could answer a few questions, that would be helpful."

"Such a shame. Patsy is a mighty fine cook. Are you sure you don't want a taste?" Gene asked.

"No, we're fine," Adam said firmly.

"Well, come on in." He gestured with a flourish for them to come inside.

Adam didn't like this one bit. He wanted to discuss this with Cheryl, but before he could say anything, she stepped around him and went further into the house. He followed after her.

The house looked exactly like the one Adam saw in his vision, minus the body parts and gore. A light blue sofa sat against the far wall. Lamps with intricate stained-glass shades sat on the end tables at either side of the sofa. Paintings of countryside landscapes decorated the walls. A painting of the house hung above the sofa. It was an eerily familiar nighttime scene. A yellow glow came from a single window upstairs. In it stood the silhouette of a woman. Cheryl noticed the picture right away and walked right up to it. Her shoes creaked on the old wood floor as she went. "What a lovely painting. Who's in the window?"

"I don't know. Patsy, I guess. Or maybe it's our resident ghost." Gene winked.

"Ghost?" Cheryl turned to look at him.

"Don't all old houses have one?" Gene continued without waiting for an answer. "A friend painted it for us. It's one of my favorites."

"You're lucky to have such a talented friend," Cheryl said.

Adam watched them closely, his pulse racing. He had to be ready for the worst.

"We're lucky in a lot of ways." Gene beamed.

Adam didn't feel particularly lucky. He was standing in a horrible place that would one day be littered with dead bodies if he did nothing to stop it from happening. "How did you know Cheryl's name earlier?"

Patsy came from the kitchen. A frilly pink apron with white polka dots was tied around her waist. Her dyed brown hair was so heavily sprayed that it stayed stationary as she moved her head. "Oh, it's so nice to have company for dinner. It's a good thing I always cook extra."

"They're here to ask about Mark," Gene said.

Patsy screwed up her face. "Who's Mark?"

Gene sighed. "You know Mark. He used to come to do odd jobs around the house." He looked at Adam and lowered his voice. "Her memory isn't what it used to be."

Patsy puckered her lips. "Oh yes. Mark was so lovely. Such a shame what happened to him."

"So you do know him?" Adam pointed at them.

"You act like hiring a handyman is a crime." Gene gave a questioning look.

Cheryl turned around, taking her attention off of the painting. "A friend of Mark's told us that you spent a lot of time with him before he died."

"That's right. We needed a lot done around the house. He replaced the gutters and took care of some plumbing problems we were having." Gene looked at Patsy for confirmation.

"I'm so glad he fixed those pipes. They used to knock so hard I thought they might break through the walls one day." Patsy chuckled.

Cheryl scowled. "He never fixed anything around our house."

"Wait," Patsy said. "Are you his wife?"

She nodded.

"Lucky you. He was so lovely. Such a charmer." Patsy blushed.

Adam and Cheryl looked at each other. "I wouldn't exactly describe him that way," Cheryl said.

"What a terrible thing to say," Gene said. "Mark would've never said anything like that about you."

Cheryl's eyes opened wide. "You've got to be kidding."

"I'm certainly not. Mark and I spent a lot of time together. We talked about you. I can't believe you walked out on him. He still loved you."

Adam watched Cheryl as Gene spoke. The muscles in her jaw and neck tensed. Her lips pulled in ever so slightly. He wondered if she would break down. She'd managed to hold it together so far.

"We're here because--" Adam stopped speaking because he saw something dark moving toward him out of the corner of his eye. He put his arm around Cheryl and pulled her toward him as he stepped out of the object's path.

"What are you doing?" Cheryl asked.

"Are you okay?" Gene asked, but the smirk on his face made Adam think that he knew exactly what was going on. Darkness rolled over the room.

"You're so jumpy," Patsy said. "Come on. Dinner is getting cold."

Adam looked over at Patsy and saw dark red blood oozing from her mouth. Her eyes were two black orbs.

Gene's face was a sunken skull, and black liquid flowed from his eyes like tears. Adam screamed. Grabbing Cheryl by the arm, he ran for the door only to find it was locked. Distant voices called to him. Cheryl was saying something, but her voice sounded far away. He tried to unlock the door, but he couldn't figure it out. In his mind, he knew the lock should be simple. Just turn the knob, but when he reached up to do it, his brain shut off. Panic gripped him. His breathing became ragged. Frantically he tried again to open the lock. Again the simple task confounded him. It was like he was attempting to solve a complicated puzzle. He couldn't understand why. Then he felt the cold water dripping on his head. He looked up to see Tanya hovering over him. Her yellow dress was the only bright thing in the darkness. Her eyes seemed to be open wide with fright. "Be careful," she said. "He's coming for you now too." She vanished. The darkness blinked away, and everything went back to normal.

"What was that all about?" Gene peered at Adam over the top of his square glasses.

Adam shook his head. "Nothing."

He looked at Cheryl, who gaped at him with a concerned expression. "Are you okay?" she asked before squirming out of his grip.

"Yeah. I'm fine." His voice was barely a whisper. "I'm just feeling a bit off. Maybe we should do this some other time." He looked at Cheryl, hoping she'd agree.

Patsy disappeared into the kitchen and came back with a tall glass of water. "Drink this. You look like you might faint." She handed him the cold glass. "Why don't you sit down for a minute?" She motioned to the sofa in the living room.

Adam held the glass in his hand. He didn't want to drink anything they offered him. Cheryl hadn't let on that she wanted to leave too, so he decided that he might take a moment to look around. "Can I use your bathroom?"

Patsy and Gene looked at each other before Gene said, "It's at the top of the stairs." He motioned to the wooden

Lady in the Lake

stairwell to his left.

The floorboards creaked under his feet as he walked up the stairs. When he got to the top, he was greeted by two doors, the bathroom and another door that was ajar. Aware that the creaky floorboards would give away his wanderings upstairs, he crept toward the door that was ajar and peered into the room.

On the floor drawn in what at first glance looked like it might be blood were two large circles, one inside the other. Inside the smallest circle the branches and roots of a tree were drawn in black. A series of white symbols marked the trunk of the tree. These symbols looked familiar to Adam, but he didn't know where he'd seen them before. Two pictures sat in the branches of the tree. One was of Patsy and the other was a man in his thirties. His face looked haggard. Adam wondered if that was Mark. He'd never seen a picture of him. Black pillar candles sat on black plates at edges of the larger circle. Adam swallowed hard. He didn't know what he was looking at, but it didn't feel right.

He tried to remain calm as he walked down the stairs with his heart racing. He followed the sound of their voices. They were in the dining room now. Cheryl sat at the dining table. Gene was talking when he walked into the room, and they all turned to look at him. He scanned their faces looking for some hint of the evil that must lie inside of them. Patsy's blue-green eyes darkened. Her eyelids drooped, and her nostrils flared. She trained her eyes on Cheryl.

"You left me for him?" Her voice was no longer shrill but deep and masculine. "Now you're back here because you think you can stop me. You can't stop me from doing anything." Her lips twisted as she spoke.

"What?" With panicked eyes, Cheryl looked back at Adam.

At that moment, Adam understood what was happening: the symbol is upstairs, the look in her eyes, the way everything had been so strange from the start.

Patsy lunged toward Cheryl, who leaped from her chair and ran toward him. They both rushed to the door. Adam looked behind him just in time to see Patsy grab a knife from the table. She charged them. This time he had to be agile. This time he had to think. There was no time for fumbling at the lock. Pushing Cheryl in front of him, they both ran to the door. Cheryl got to it first and unlocked it. Adam turned around and hit Patsy but not before she sliced into his arm with her knife. He yelled in agony. He had to ignore the pain. "Go! Go!" he yelled at Cheryl.

They ran out the door and down the porch steps to their rental car. They got into the car and slammed the doors just as Gene and Patsy reached them. They pounded on the hood as they backed out of the driveway. They drove the bumpy twisting road as quickly as they could, kicking up dirt as they went. They'd solved the case. They just needed to tell the police, but what to tell them?

Chapter 19

Cheryl twisted around in her seat. She expected to see Gene and Patsy tearing after them in their shiny black sedan, but the road behind them was empty. Even though they weren't chasing them, she knew she could never truly be safe until whatever allowed Mark to inhibit other people's bodies was undone. She sat back down in her seat, her heart racing.

"When I went to the bathroom, I looked in one of the rooms upstairs, and it looked like they'd been doing some kind of ritual before we arrived." Adam spoke much faster than usual.

"What do you mean?" Cheryl's mind was so busy that she had difficulty focusing on what he was saying.

"There were symbols drawn on the floor in one of the rooms, with candles, and pictures. I don't really know about that stuff, but it looked pretty creepy to me." He didn't stop at the stop sign at the end of the road. There was no reason to; nothing was coming. The tires squealed as he made a hard right onto the main road.

Cheryl turned and looked behind them again. Still no one followed them. She knew it didn't matter because she'd seen that Mark didn't have to follow her physically. He could inhabit the body of anyone around her. She looked over at Adam and wondered what would happen if Mark suddenly took his body over. "It has been Mark this whole time." She reached her hand in her coat pocket and felt the plastic baggie of powder. She'd meant to use it, but everything had happened so fast that she couldn't. Next time she needed to be ready.

Adam was visibly distraught. "We were right. Tanya was telling us the whole time." He sped up the road toward downtown, but she didn't want to stay in town anymore.

Cheryl wondered if Adam knew where he was going because she had no idea. It didn't take long before police lights flashed in their rearview mirror.

"I guess we don't have to go to the station." Adam slowed and pulled onto the shoulder of the road.

The officer swaggered up to the driver's side window. Adam already had the license and registration ready to hand him.

"Do you know how fast you were going?" the officer asked, his eyes shifting back and forth between them as he spoke.

"I'm sorry. I know I was speeding." Adam handed him his information.

The officer narrowed his eyes at them before taking it. "Sit tight. I'll be right back." He looked down at Adam's driver's license.

They sat in the car in silence, both watching the police officer in the mirror. A second police car drove up and pulled over on the shoulder in front of them. Two police officers got out of the car in front of them with their guns drawn, pointing at them. The officer in the car behind them got out too, holding his gun straight out in front of him. They were all yelling commands at them.

Cheryl twisted around to see a police officer with his gun drawn approaching the car. "What's happening?" she screeched.

"Put your hands up where they can see them," Adam instructed.

The police officer was yelling, his face red and voice strained. "Get out of the car! Keep your hands up!"

Cheryl's heart raced. Adrenaline surged through her. They both reached down and slowly opened their doors, their hands high in the air.

"Get down on your knees! Hands behind your head!" The officer kept moving forward with his gun drawn.

On her knees, Cheryl couldn't see Adam or what was happening on the other side of the car. She could only see a police officer rushing toward her. Tears streamed down her face. "I don't know what's going on. What did I do wrong?"

The cold metal handcuffs snapped around her wrist, and her arms were being pulled up and back, forcing her to her feet. "I don't understand what's happening. You can't just arrest us like this."

"It's going to be okay," Adam said from the other side of the car. His right cheek was red and swollen.

It wasn't going to be okay. No matter what he said, she knew he was wrong.

"Cheryl Hampton," the officer began. "You're under arrest for the murder of Ashely Winter."

"What?" Cheryl yelled. "I didn't kill anyone!"

The officer ignored her and continued. "You have the right to remain silent..."

Cheryl couldn't hear anything else he said. It was like she was swimming through molasses. Everything slowed down, including the officer's voice, which sounded like it was being played back to her at slow speed. "Wait." She finally managed to say. "I didn't kill anyone. I'm here to help you find the killer."

He spoke right over her protests.

She looked for Adam, who was saying something to her, but she couldn't quite make out what. The police officer pushed her, forcing her to move forward toward his car. He yanked open the back door and shoved her inside. She expected Adam to join her in the back seat of the police cruiser, but when she looked up, she saw that he was being led to the other car. He was talking the whole time. She wondered what he was saying. Was he asking questions? Was he demanding justice? As the officer put his meaty hand on Adam's head to get him into the car, Cheryl noticed Tanya standing on the hood of the police cruiser, water rushing down her like she was standing under a waterfall. She held her hands out toward Cheryl before melting into a puddle herself and disappearing. Cheryl felt like she was being pulled apart by madness.

When the police officers got back into the car, she started talking immediately. "How can you arrest us? What evidence do you have?"

"We'll talk about that at the station," the officer said.

"I've only been here a few days. We just came because we were looking into the murders. The first day we showed up at the police station, we talked to Detective Haskell. You can even ask him." As she was talking, she realized that what she was saying wasn't evidence of anything, but she couldn't stop. She wanted to explain herself.

"You'll talk to Detective Haskell when you get to the station," the officer said with a flat monotone voice. Cheryl felt like they weren't even listening to her.

"We're trying to solve the case too. Don't you get it?"

He didn't respond. Realizing that explaining this to him was useless, she sat back in the car. She tried to relax and watch the passing scenery instead of worrying about what

Lady in the Lake

was to come. She had no idea what she could do about it anyway.

**

Adam asked questions but didn't get answers. When they rolled up to the police station, Cheryl was already being pulled from her police car. He saw the look of terror in her eyes as she looked around. He never thought when he suggested that they go ahead with this trip, they would end up like this.

"Get out of the car," the cop said, reaching down and grabbing Adam by the upper arm. He yanked him out of the car, wrenching his shoulder.

"We haven't done anything." He'd already said that more times than he could count in the car. It was all he could think to say.

"You all say that." The police officer smirked. "Nobody I've ever arrested has been guilty."

Adam knew it was better not to say anything back. As they went inside, he kept his eyes peeled, looking for Cheryl but didn't see her anywhere. The officer he was with led him straight to a small room like the one they had met Detective Haskell in only a few days before, but this time he was in handcuffs.

"Sit down." The officer motioned to a chair.

Adam sat. The officer slammed the door closed, leaving him sitting with his hands still cuffed behind his back. Where was Cheryl? He waited in that room for what felt like hours. He studied the fake wood grain on the tabletop. The lines were much too uniform to be natural.

Finally, after what seemed like an eternity, he heard a key in the lock. Detective Haskell walked in with a white Styrofoam cup in his hand. "I brought you some coffee." He put the cup down on the table and reached into his pocket and pulled out a key ring to undo Adam's handcuffs.

Blood rushed back into Adam's hands. He rubbed his wrists. "Why am I here? I haven't done anything."

"Haven't you?" He took a long drag on his cigarette. "You and your girlfriend have been playing an interesting little game. You waltz in here, announcing that you know who the killer is. Then you find a new victim that we didn't even know about." He took another drag from his cigarette before flicking the ashes onto the floor.

"You dug up the spot?" When Adam called Detective Haskell, he didn't expect him to check out the area at all. He didn't sound like he was interested. "Did you find her?"

"Oh yes, we found her. That's what you had planned, wasn't it?" He took another drag on his cigarette.

Adam was pretty sure he wasn't allowed to smoke in the police station but knew asking about it was a bad idea.

Smoke seeped out of Detective Haskell's mouth with his words. "I don't know what it is with your kind of people. You think you're so smart you can lay all the evidence out in front of us, and we wouldn't catch on."

It was then that Adam realized the weight of what was happening. "You think we killed her?"

"How else would you even know she was missing?" The detective stepped into the room completely now, letting the door close behind him. "I don't know what your dark, twisted game is, but I'm on to you." He held his cigarette between two fingers and pointed it at him.

Adam's blood ran cold. "You've got this all wrong. We're trying to solve this case just like you are. That's why we came."

Detective Haskell took a few steps closer to Adam. Putting his hands on the table, he leaned over to get closer to him. "Really? Because everything I looked at says that I've got this right."

Adam couldn't believe what was happening, but looking back on all the circumstances, he should have known. He couldn't let them arrest him and Cheryl for something neither of them did. He'd made her get involved with the hope that he could help her put away her past hurt and move on with life. He had to admit that selfishly he hoped it would help her move on with him. If they ended up in jail for murder, it would be his fault. "Mark Hampton did all of this." There was no way to back up this statement, but he said it anyway.

"Mark Hampton is dead." He slammed his fist down on the table, and Adam almost jumped out of his skin. "That's right. I looked him up since your girlfriend keeps mentioning him. He's been dead for more than a year. I'm tired of these games."

"I want to talk to Cheryl."

"I want a billion dollars and a yacht. It doesn't matter what you want." He yanked the chair out from under the table and sat down across from Adam. "I want to catch this serial killer so people in my community will stop dying."

"I'm not a serial killer."

He ground out his cigarette on the leg of his chair. "I never said you were. I checked. You were in Florida until just a few days ago. Just because you didn't kill all those other people doesn't mean you didn't kill this one." He laid the squashed cigarette butt on the table and sat back in his chair. "So tell me about Ashley Winter. Why her?"

"I don't know anything about Ashley Winter."

"Except you killed her and buried her in a field." His face twitched, the muscles tightening around his right eye. He blinked a few times and looked down at the table before raising his cold gaze back to Adam. "Like you and Cheryl are going to be soon."

"What?" Adam was sure he had misheard.

Detective Haskell's face relaxed. "You can deny this all you want, but we will find the truth."

"What did you just say before about Cheryl and me?" Adam's heart thumped loudly in his chest.

"I said we're going to figure out exactly what happened sooner or later, so you might as well make it easy on yourself and confess." He stood up. He took the crushed cigarette butt from the table and put it in the pocket of his pants.

"What was that thing about Cheryl and me ending up buried in a field?" He had been threatening them. Adam heard it and hoped someone was on the other side of the mirror to hear it too.

"I'll be back. Why don't you sit here and think about whether or not you're ready to tell me what really happened?" He opened the door, letting in the buzz of the police station. "If you make this easy for me, I'll do what I can to make it easier for you." He stepped out of the room, and the door clicked closed behind him. Adam heard a key jiggle in the lock before he walked away. This wasn't going to be easy for anyone. Adam knew Mark would make sure of that.

Chapter 20

Cheryl perched on the edge of her chair, her hands still cuffed behind her back. The room was warm, and she was starting to sweat in her winter coat. The door swung open, and Detective Haskell stood in the doorway. "You can't stay out of trouble, can you?" His lips curled into that familiar sneer, knocking the wind out of her.

She gasped. "I haven't done anything wrong." She spoke as if the man standing in front of her was indeed Detective Haskell, even though she knew he wasn't.

He stepped into the room, closing the door behind him. Cheryl looked at the mirrored wall. She hoped someone was watching, but she knew in all likelihood, they weren't.

His hard-soled shoes clicked on the tile floor as he walked toward her. She recognized the slow gait. "You pick up and walk out on me without a word. No note. No phone call." The words slid from his mouth. "I thought we had something special. I thought we were in love. Apparently, love doesn't mean anything to you. And now you come waltzing back into town trying to ruin my plans all over again." He walked around the table and stood behind Cheryl.

She struggled with her cuffs, but that only seemed to make them tighter.

He put his hands on her shoulders. They were heavy. The

webbing between his thumbs and index fingers touched the base of her neck. His fingers pushed into her collarbones. She closed her eyes and focused, trying her best not to show her fear. She'd been in this position so many times before. "Mark?"

He inhaled through his clenched teeth, making a hissing sound. "Yes, baby." He tightened his grip on her shoulders, pressing his fingertips harder into her flash. "It's me. You didn't think you could get away from me so easily, did you?" He let go of her shoulders abruptly, his arms swinging out to the side in a grand gesture. He walked around the table, pulled out the chair across from her, and sat down. "You destroyed me when you left. I thought I was never going to see you again. Can you imagine what that was like? The love of your life up and disappearing one day."

Cheryl shook her head. She wondered what would happen if she screamed. Would someone come into the room to save her?

"I tried to find girls to take your place, but none of them were you. They were too loud or too quiet or too bossy or too timid. I didn't want all that. I was looking for someone just right, like you." He dragged his fingernails across the desk. "You can't trust a woman as far as you can throw her." He laughed dryly. "And that's not far. God knows I've tried."

Cheryl wondered what he meant but dared not ask. Her gaze kept shifting to the door. The law was just outside, and yet she might still die in this room. She thought that she should keep him talking. He had always liked explaining himself, especially if she made him feel smart. "Those women, the ones they found dead, you killed them, didn't you?"

He grinned and leaned back in his chair. "If you're asking me if I'm the Ridge Point Killer, you're right. That's me. In

Lady in the Lake

the flesh." He cackled and looked down at his chest. "This one's not that bad. I've had better, but I think a cop is a good choice." He turned his head back and forth as if trying out his new body for the first time. His neck cracked. "This one will do just fine. Maybe I'll leave a bit of evidence around, so they catch him."

Cheryl narrowed her eyes at him. "So you've been killing these women to get back at me."

He threw his head back and laughed loudly. "You haven't changed. You think an awful lot of yourself. Not everything has to do with you."

"But you just said--"

"You don't have to tell me what I just said. I know what I said." He struck the tabletop with his fist. "If you listened for a change, you'd know what I was saying, or are you just too stupid to understand? This is about me and what I want to do. Someone as weak as you doesn't know what it's like to feel in control. You don't know true power, but I do. The first time I pushed that girl under the water, I felt it. Fighting back, she scratched me, but I held her under until her body went limp. The life floated out of her. I felt it drift away. I did that. Do you know what that's like?"

Cheryl shook her head.

"That's because you're weak." He leaned his chair back, lifting the front legs off the ground. "Do you remember the night I stabbed you? I was drunk, but I knew what I was doing. The knife went into your gut like butter. I was so surprised that I think I went into shock. They'd told me that was what it would be like, but I didn't really believe it. You were supposed to be my first, but I messed it all up." He stood up, and Cheryl wondered if he would come around the table again. Would this be the moment that he slipped his hands around her neck and choked the life out of her too?

"Who told you? What did you mess up?"

"Your first sacrifice has to be someone special, or else the ritual won't work. The first one has to be someone you love. Someone who loves you." He stood behind her.

"Sacrifice? Was Tanya Garret a sacrifice? What about the others? What about your accident?" She nervously chewed the inside of her cheek, waiting for his answer.

He walked to the side of the room so she could see him now. "That was no accident. That was part of the ritual. First, I needed to sacrifice someone else and then myself. You can't gain anything without sacrifice." He shoved his hands into his pockets and rocked back on his heels. He was so relaxed.

Cheryl wondered what it was like to feel untouchable. She wondered how much it would surprise him when she was finally able to cut him down to size. If only she could get her hand into her pocket and get to the banishing powder. "And the people in the house, Patsy and Gene?" She felt like she knew the answer but wanted to hear it from him.

"Gene taught me everything I ever needed to--" He turned and looked at the door just as it swung open.

A broad-faced police detective walked in. He mopped the sweat from his forehead with a white handkerchief. Detective Haskell's shoulders slumped, and he looked at the floor. It was almost as if she could see Mark leave his body. His demeanor changed almost immediately. The cocky swagger was gone, replaced by Detective Haskell's edge. He looked around the room, and she recognized the confusion on his face.

"I'm going to let you handle the questioning, Spencer." Detective Haskell looked like he might fall over. His skin was pale, and his eyes vacant.

"Are you okay?" Spencer looked him over with a concerned expression on his face.

Detective Haskell waved his hand dismissively. "Yeah. Go

ahead. I'll watch for a few minutes."

"Okay." Spencer turned his attention to Cheryl. "I'm Detective Spencer. I just have a few questions for you." He removed her handcuffs before sitting across from her.

"Okay."

"What was the nature of your relationship with Ashley Winter?" Detective Spencer began pulling pictures out of a folder and lining them up on the table in front of her. The first picture was of a smiling dark-haired woman in her early twenties. She stood smiling at a canyon's edge, her nose slightly sunburnt. The next picture was a corpse. The gaping mouth was packed with soil. Cheryl immediately recognized the wound on the side of her head. She could only look at the picture for a few seconds before looking away.

"I don't have a relationship with her. I've never met her before." She was already trying to figure out how to explain any of this. It was hard enough to explain to people who wanted to believe. She never expected to have to explain her abilities to law enforcement.

"How did you know where she was buried or even that she was dead at all?" He put his fingers on the edges of both the photos and pushed them across the table toward her.

Cheryl looked at his face refusing to look at the pictures again. The whole time she remembered Detective Haskell was standing in the corner near the door, still looking stunned. She wondered what he was thinking. "We had an accident in our car, and it was taken to that lot. I thought I saw something strange in the field when we were cleaning out our car. I just went for a little walk to check it out and found the clearing of snow. It looked like someone had been digging there." She knew the story was farfetched, but what else could she say?

"What did you see in the field that seemed so unusual?" Detective Spencer asked.

Detective Haskell was moving around now. He walked slowly up to the table where she sat.

Cheryl cleared her throat and watched him as she spoke. "Adam was cleaning out the car. We had just been in an accident, but you probably already know that."

Detective Spencer flipped to a page in his folder. "It's been an eventful day for you. It says here that the driver Adam Green was taken in for questioning."

"I guess. I really don't know what happened because I went to the hospital." She watched Detective Haskell, who stood with his hand on the table like he was trying to steady himself. "Anyway, when Adam was getting this stuff out of the car, I was feeling a bit antsy." She was definitely not ready to tell them that she saw ghosts. She knew it wouldn't help her case. It might even make it worse. "I decided to go for a little walk around. I walked up into the field because I saw something strange. There was a place where the snow wasn't as deep as everyplace else. When I got up there, it looked like someone had recently dug a hole."

Detective Spencer tapped his finger on the table and looked at her for what felt like forever before continuing. "So, what you're telling me is that you just saw that the ground had been disturbed there and solely from that you decided there must be a body buried there. Not only did you decide that there must be a body buried there, but you also knew that body belonged to Ashley Winter. Can you see how this doesn't make sense?"

"Yes." Cheryl had no idea how to explain herself. She wondered what Adam had told them. "I know it sounds strange, but I promise you that's what happened."

"How did you know Ashley Winter was missing?" He stared at her waiting for an answer she couldn't give.

"I don't know." She had no idea if this was the right thing

Lady in the Lake

to do. What could possibly be the right thing to do in this situation? She wished she could make a phone call and talk to Day. She always had good advice for Cheryl. She wondered what was happening with Adam. What was he telling them?

"This is what it sounds like to me." Detective Spencer paused to flip through pages in his folder. He pointed to the picture of Ashley Winter. "You and Ashley already knew each other. I don't know how but I'll figure that part out. You get angry at her, so you arrange to have your boyfriend who's in the next room help you kill her and bury her."

"I didn't know her before. We didn't kill her. Whoever the Ridge Point Killer is did this." Her words were more emphatic now.

"You've said nothing to convince me otherwise. As a matter of fact, I think that you might be the Ridge Point Killer or at least know who the killer is. Maybe you and your boyfriend have been going around and killing people here for months."

"That's impossible. We've only been here for a few days. Call our friends they'll tell you." Cheryl pretended not to be nervous, but she was quaking inside. What if she ended up in jail for the rest of her life? What would happen then?

Detective Spencer took the pictures of Ashley off the table and stuck them in his folder before snapping it shut. "This is your last chance to confess. If you do, I might be able to convince the prosecutor to go easy on you."

"There's no way they're going to go easy on a serial killer." After Cheryl spoke, she knew she probably should've kept her mouth shut.

"So you're saying you're a serial killer?" There was a glint in his eye when he thought he had caught her.

"No. I'm saying that you think I'm a serial killer, so there is no way that anyone would really be lenient with me. I haven't killed anyone. The only thing I've done wrong here is--" She stopped herself.

"Go on then. I want to know what you've done wrong." He tilted his head at her and waited.

Cheryl decided she had nothing to lose. She could either tell the truth, or she could end up in jail. "I saw Ashley Winter in a vision. That happens to me a lot. I see ghosts, and they tell me things. Usually, they tell me simple things, like to say goodbye to the kids for them or to tell their wife where they stashed some extra money. I don't get all caught up in murders like this. Luckily, most people die of natural causes or in an accident. They don't get drowned in a lake or their head beaten in by the ghost of my ex-husband." She didn't know whether to laugh or cry at that bit. So instead, she plowed forward because Detective Spencer was not interrupting her. "While we were dealing with things with the car, I saw Ashley Winter in the woman's bathroom. She told me that she was murdered, and then she showed me where she was buried. That's why I went over there. That's how I knew who was buried there. It's not just her though. The whole reason I'm here is that Tanya Garrett has been appearing to me too. She's actually been terrorizing me, to tell the truth."

Detective Spencer frowned. He didn't believe her. She didn't blame him. She wouldn't have believed herself either.

She continued her story. "My ex-husband, Mark, died, but he was involved in some kind of cult or something. I'm not sure what. I don't even know if it matters. I do know that he's been taking over people's bodies since he's died. He's your serial killer. He killed Tanya Garrett and Ashley Winter and all of the people that have turned up dead in this town recently. I know it."

Detective Spencer drew his eyebrows together and gave Detective Haskell a sidelong glance. Detective Haskell looked at the floor.

"Just ask him," Cheryl said. "He knows. He's experienced it."

Detective Haskell raised his gaze to hers but said nothing.

"Can you believe this?" Detective Spencer pointed at Cheryl with his pen. The chair scraped the floor as he stood. "I'll be back to talk to you when you're ready to tell the truth." He marched to the door and pulled it open. He looked at Detective Haskell.

"Go ahead," Detective Haskell said. "I have a few more questions I want to ask her." As he spoke, he seemed to have regained his confidence.

Detective Spencer left the room, letting the door fall closed behind him.

Detective Haskell sat down in the chair across from Cheryl, staring at her in silence. He looked to the left toward the mirrored wall before leaning across the table and finally speaking. "What just happened to me?"

Relief washed over Cheryl. He would believe her. Mark had been trying to scare her but had accidentally helped her.

Chapter 21

As the adrenaline wore off, Adam's head began to throb. He leaned forward, resting it on the table in front of him. Where was Cheryl? What was happening? How was he going to get them out of this? Adam ran through the incidents that got them into this situation. What could they have done differently? He wasn't sure.

A drop of water ran across the tabletop, meeting the skin on his hand. Adam looked up to see Tanya Garrett sitting across from him. He straightened up in his chair and glanced at the mirror, always aware that someone could be watching. She looked different now. The bruising around her eyes was gone, and he thought he might be able to see some joy in her face. Water streamed down her in ribbons. She put her palms flat on the tabletop and leaned in.

"He's here," she whispered before vanishing like smoke.

The door opened, and Detective Spencer walked in, carrying a small digital recorder. "We need to record your confession." He locked the door behind him.

"I haven't confessed to anything."

Detective Spencer snorted. "Your girlfriend has. She's saying this was all your idea."

"She would never do that." How naïve did he think he was? He'd seen this routine plenty of times before in movies.

"Really? She told me you were the one who wanted to kill Ashley Winter." He paused and looked down at the recorder. "But we both know that this wasn't your idea. She was the mastermind all along, wasn't she? I'm on your side. I don't want to see you go down for something you didn't do."

Adam shook his head. "She would never say that. I don't believe you. Lying to me to get me to confess to something I didn't do can't be legal." He looked at the recorder and then back up at Detective Spencer. "Let me talk to Cheryl."

"That's not the way things work here." Detective Spencer shifted in his chair, and his breathing grew raspy. His face turned red, and he stretched his neck long. "Now you're going to--" His head lolled, and his eyes rolled back for a moment. He snapped his head forward, and this time he had a whole new demeanor. It was as if he had become someone else. He turned a bit, spreading his legs wide and hooking his arm over the back of the chair. "So, what do you think you're doing here?"

Adam grimaced. "Like I told you before, I came here from Florida because I have information about the murder of Tanya Garrett. I want to bring her killer to justice."

Detective Spencer sneered. "Justice doesn't exist. If it did, that bitch wouldn't still be walking around. She convinced you that she could stop me, didn't she?"

"Mark?" Adam asked.

"In the flesh." He cackled. "Do you think she would care if you turned up dead?" He shrugged casually. "She's a cold woman, but she might surprise me. I figure it's worth testing to see what would happen."

Adam looked at the door. To get to it, he would have to run past Mark, and Mark had a weapon. As soon as the gun went off, this room would be swarming with police, but by then it would already be too late.

**

Cheryl leaned across the table at Detective Haskell. "This is going to sound crazy." Even though she could see that he was ready to believe her, she felt the need to preface what she said.

"Right now, you can tell me anything. I feel like I've gone crazy."

She was so excited to talk that he had barely finished his sentence when she started to explain. "The serial killer you've been looking for is already dead. That's why you haven't been able to catch him. He takes over someone's body and makes that person kill his target before he moves on."

"How is that even possible?" Detective Haskell sat back in his chair.

"I think he was inside you just a few moments ago." Her eyes searched his face to see if he believed her.

"I know. I was saying things and doing things that I had no control over. I could see what was happening, but I felt like I was watching from a distance. That was him?"

"That was him." Relief settled into her. "He wants to kill me and..." Suddenly she realized that if he was in the building, he could be going after Adam right now. "Where's Adam?"

Detective Haskell shot up out of his seat and rushed to the door. She didn't have to explain what she was thinking because he was thinking the same. Cheryl followed him to the door, fully expecting him to stop her. She was happy when he didn't. Maybe this meant she was no longer under arrest.

People walked back and forth in the station. None of them knew that evil walked among them. The realization that Mark could take over any one of these people overwhelmed Cheryl. She stayed close on Detective Haskell's heels as he ran

Lady in the Lake

to the door just three doors up from the room she had been in. He tried the knob, and it was locked. He pulled the keys from his pocket and unlocked it.

**

Adam leaped from his chair across the table at Mark, knocking him to the ground. He knew he had to fight if he wanted to survive. He couldn't give Mark the time to get to the detective's gun. Then it would all be over. They struggled on the floor. Detective Spencer was bigger than Adam, stronger, but Adam was agile, wiry, and determined.

He knew the secret was to act quickly and decisively. As soon as they hit the floor, he began to punch the detective, hoping to disorient him so much that he couldn't find his weapon. He knew this was dangerous. At any moment, someone could come into the room behind the mirror or into the room itself and see him fighting with a cop. That would almost guarantee jail time or even get him shot, but he was not going to let Mark Hampton win.

Even with all the fight in him and the element of surprise, size and strength were still too much. Mark managed to flip him over, penning Adam to the floor. Adam put his hands around his neck, choking him. The detective grabbed Adam's neck too, giving up on the idea of getting his gun. Adam gasped for air. He wondered who would suffocate first. The door burst open just as Mark passed out, his heavy bulk falling on Adam blocking his vision. Adam couldn't see who came into the room and was certain he would end up in jail for the rest of his life.

Whomever it was rolled Detective Spencer off of him. It was Detective Haskell and Cheryl. Detective Spencer opened his eyes. "What happened?" he asked groggily. He sat up and looked around the room bleary-eyed.

Cheryl squatted down in front of Adam.

He flung his arms around her and held onto her tight. "Thank God, you're safe." He looked at Detective Spencer, who was sitting on the floor, rubbing his head. "Mark's here."

"I know." Cheryl looked at Detective Haskell. "He's jumping around from body to body. He was just in Detective Haskell."

Adam also looked at the detective. If Mark could enter someone's body with such ease, there was nothing stopping him from taking over Cheryl or Adam. He was certain of that and wondered what he could do to resist such a takeover. "Does that mean you believe us now?"

Detective Haskell helped Detective Spencer off the floor and into a chair. Detective Spencer rubbed his neck. "I don't know what just happened. One minute everything was normal and the next..." He shook his head slowly and found his way to his feet. "I need a minute." He motioned to the door.

Detective Haskell pulled the door open. "I'll be right back," he said to Cheryl.

Both of them stepped outside, leaving Cheryl and Adam alone.

"I thought I was dead for sure." Adam ran his fingers through his hair.

Cheryl reached out and touched his neck, where Detective Spencer's hands had previously been wrapped around it, choking the life out of him. She bit her lip and creased her forehead. "It happened to Detective Haskell too. He didn't try to kill me. He just threatened to." She sat down in the chair. "He remembers what happened. He said it was like observing himself threatening me." She glanced over at the mirror before leaning in closer to Adam. "I think he believes us."

Lady in the Lake

Before Adam had time to respond, the door opened and Detective Haskell walked in.

"Is he all right?" Cheryl asked.

"Detective Spencer? He'll be fine. He says he doesn't remember anything. He thinks he just blacked out. He's going home for the day." He looked at both of them. "Is this real?"

"Unfortunately, it is," Cheryl said.

Detective Haskell motioned to the chairs. "We need to talk. Tell me everything."

Cheryl started from the beginning when she first started seeing Tanya Garrett. She explained why they came there and her relationship with Mark. Detective Haskell stood with his arms crossed over his chest, pressing his lips into a fine line as he listened. When she finally stopped speaking, he looked at the floor while thumping his chest with his thumb.

They watched him in silence, waiting for him to respond.

"I'm not a superstitious guy," he finally said. "I go to Christmas mass, and sometimes I go on Easter Sunday too, but that's it. Religion was never my thing, but that's not to say that I don't believe in God or the devil..." He raised his gaze over their heads to look at the wall for a minute. "What I felt tonight certainly did feel like the devil."

"Sometimes I felt like Mark was the devil too," Cheryl said, "but he's not. He might've made a pact with the devil though."

"I didn't know that was a real thing," Detective Haskell said.

"He is definitely your killer. If people can remember what happened when he was in their bodies, then you have a lot of traumatized people walking around who should've turned themselves in." Cheryl bit her lip. "Hopefully, most of them are like Detective Spencer and can't remember a thing after it happens."

Detective Haskell nodded. "That's a more likely story." He

turned his attention to Adam. "So this is what you guys do?"

"Kind of," Adam said. "We deal with more haunted-house stuff."

"So what do we do to stop this?" His gaze bounced back and forth between them.

"We're not sure." Cheryl never had a problem with admitting that she didn't know something.

"Have you been back to the house by the lake?" Adam asked.

Detective Haskell shook his head. "No. We told Tanya's mother that we would search the lake soon."

"We went there." Adam was ready to tell him everything he knew too. "I saw something strange when we were there."

"You shouldn't have gone there," Detective Haskell snapped.

"We know Tanya's body is in the lake, and we needed to do something. You weren't willing to help." Cheryl jabbed him with her words.

"But you can't decide you're going to be part of an active police investigation," he replied.

"You weren't investigating." Cheryl raised her voice. "If you had been investigating, we wouldn't have had to go over there. If you'd searched the lake like I'd asked, you would've found Tanya Garrett's body, but even after her mother called, you still haven't done it."

"We are doing everything we can to stop this. That's why we went over there even though we knew it was dangerous," Adam said. "We came here to help you, and you didn't want our help, so we decided to act on our own."

"You can't expect us to respond to every crazy idea someone calls with. We have to act on credible tips. When you came to us, what you said didn't seem like a credible tip. You can't blame me for not believing you. If you were me, would you have believed your story?" Detective Haskell's voice rose.

Adam knew he wouldn't have. Before any of this happened to him, he didn't believe stories like this either. "You believe us now though. So that means you'll help us, right?"

Detective Haskell nodded. "I'll do what I can, but I can't make any promises about anyone else on the force. How do we stop this?"

"I think this all stops at Gene and Patsy's house." Cheryl knew as much as Adam did but seemed more confident about this. "They're helping him do this somehow. If we can stop them, I think we can stop Mark too."

Chapter 22

When they knocked, no one answered, but Gene and Patsy's black sedan sat in the driveway. Even though Detective Haskell agreed to let them go with him to the house, Cheryl could still tell he was suspicious of them. He stood behind them at the front door, focusing on all of their movements. She could feel his glare and wondered what he thought they might do.

She reached for the brass knocker again. It thumped loudly.

"Maybe they're not there," Detective Haskell said.

"They're there. I can feel it." Cheryl's entire body tingled with danger.

They stood together on the porch for a few minutes. The setting sun gave the sky a dusty pink glow. The trees transformed into dark skeletal silhouettes. Cheryl could see her breath, a puff of white smoke as she stood anxiously watching the door. She looked at the doorknob, waiting to see it turn.

"I'm going to walk around the back and see if I see anything." Detective Haskell turned and walked down the three porch steps. Then he turned back and looked at them as if realizing they were still supposed to be suspects, and he shouldn't leave them alone. "You should come with me."

Lady in the Lake

"What if someone comes to the door?" Adam asked.

"They won't." Detective Haskell's answer was so definitive that Cheryl wondered how he knew.

As they walked around the house, Detective Haskell tried to peer into windows, but they were all covered, the blinds tightly drawn. It was like the house itself was sleeping.

The back door was white with a frosted window at the top. Detective Haskell motioned for Cheryl to go up to it.

"Do you want me to knock?" she asked, nearly stumbling on a hole in the grass as she walked over to the cement pad by the door.

Detective Haskell shook his head. "Just try the knob and see if it will open."

Cheryl didn't like the idea of this at all. She would never just walk into someone's house. Cautiously she walked up to the door, wondering if someone was on the other side watching the shadow she cast on the frosted glass. Her heart pumped, and her chest tightened, making it difficult for her to inhale. With a shaky hand, she reached for the doorknob and turned it. The door eased open a crack. Cheryl turned and looked over her shoulder at Detective Haskell and Adam.

"It opened," she whispered, hunching over as she spoke, like bad posture would make her less noticeable to whatever waited for them inside.

Detective Haskell and Adam hurried to the door. Detective Haskell pulled his gun from the holster and held it up like the police always did in movies. He pushed the door open with his foot. "Police!" he announced.

"I guess we're not trying to surprise them." Cheryl followed him inside.

"I'm sure he knows what he's doing," Adam said.

Detective Haskell ignored them and kept moving forward. They were in a mudroom with coats hanging in a line on the hooks on the wall. Cheryl counted five. Who did they all belong to? They passed through a doorway into the kitchen where a long rectangular table sat at the end closest to them. The mismatched wooden chairs were all pushed in, some with rounded backs, others squared. There were place settings at each chair, a meal for six. The savory scent of a pot roast filled Cheryl's nostrils. Beneath that smell, there was another, something sweet in an unpleasant way. Cheryl sniffed. "Do you smell that?" Detective Haskell had moved beyond them now into the living room.

Adam gave Cheryl a little shove. "We need to make sure we stay with him."

She hurried into the living room with Adam behind her. Fear ratcheted through her. She reached her hand back to Adam, who put his fingers around hers.

A thud shattered the eerie silence of the house. Detective Haskell turned, pointing his gun toward the staircase. He moved forward cautiously, his gun extended out in front of him. They crept up the stairs together.

Cheryl stepped up to the first step and then looked up the staircase. Ashley and Tanya stood together at the top. "They're here," Cheryl whispered.

"I know," Detective Haskell said, but he didn't know. He had no idea who she was talking about.

"Tanya and Ashley are at the top of the stairs. Can you see them?" she whispered to Adam.

He held his fingers to his lips, telling her to be quiet as they ascended the stairs. Cheryl focused on the ghosts, hoping they would tell her what to do next, but they only watched in silence until Detective Haskell walked through them, and their forms dissipated like smoke. Detective Haskell stood against the wall by the closed door at the top of the stairs. A low rumble that sounded like a combination of something human

Lady in the Lake

and something mechanical seeped through the walls, vibrating in Cheryl's chest. She pressed her back against the wall next to Detective Haskell. Even though she'd been afraid of guns her whole life, she found herself wishing for one now. She looked at Adam, who stood silently beside her and wondered if he was afraid too.

She looked back at Detective Haskell. She could see how his chest and shoulders rose and fell with his breath. She swore she could see the quickening rhythm of his pulse in his neck. He looked back at them and nodded. "Stay here," he mouthed. He reached out and turned the doorknob. The hinges creaked as the door yawned open. Nothing came out. The rumbling didn't stop, and from where Cheryl was, she couldn't see anything inside the room. Detective Haskell jumped in front of the doorway with his gun outstretched and froze. A chorus of chanting rose in the air accompanied by the angry squawking of a bird and the fierce beating of wings.

Cheryl and Adam waited for Detective Haskell to move. The longer he stood perfectly still, the more unnerved they felt. "Detective," Adam finally said. He walked around Cheryl to the doorway.

When he looked inside the room, his eyes widened, and he stood frozen in time. Cheryl didn't want to know what he saw, but she knew what she wanted didn't matter. She'd have no choice.

**

Adam had learned a lot of things since he'd met Cheryl. He'd learned that ghosts are real and that monsters exist. He learned that sometimes the dead don't know they're dead and that sometimes they do, but they just don't want to give up their lives so quickly. Even with all that he did know and everything he'd seen, he wasn't prepared for what he saw when he looked through that doorway.

The room was larger than he remembered. On the floor painted in white were the same shapes and symbols as before. People dressed in long white robes stood along the edges of the room in a line, flanking the walls. Blank white masks covered their faces. A pile of bones lay in the middle of the room: a skull, a femur, a ribcage. They were not arranged to form a person but lay in a pile like discarded scraps.

The symbols on the floor, the people standing on the edges of the room, the bones were all strange, but those weren't what stopped Adam in his tracks. Those weren't what made him wonder about life and the world he lived in. What did was the creature standing behind the bones. It was like something he'd never seen before. The beast stood so tall that it had to hunch over, so its head didn't hit the ceiling. It's flesh looked to have been singed away, revealing sinewy muscles sheathed in fibrous white layers of tissue. Red and pink showed through crisp blackened edges of what was once skin. The creature's face looked like it had been hastily assembled. The nose was crooked. The mouth was so wide it nearly split its face in half, and there were three eyes where there should've been two.

When it saw Adam, it opened its great mouth, the top of its head flipping back like a candy dispenser and its long forked tongue unfurling. It roared, and Adam realized that the creature standing before him was the source of the low rumble they'd heard upon entering the house. Looking at it had the same effect on him as it must've had on Detective Haskell because even though he wanted to run, even though every part of him told him that safety was somewhere far, far from here, he stayed absolutely still. The fear coursing through him anchored his feet to the ground.

Lady in the Lake

People standing along the walls swayed back and forth, whispering something in unison. Adam tried to turn his head, to look at Cheryl, to tell her to run, but not a single muscle in his body would move. The floor beneath him began to vibrate, making the nerves in his feet buzz.

"What's happening?" Cheryl reached out her hand and grabbed hold of his forearm.

She stepped toward him, one foot and then another. Time slowed to a crawl.

He wished he could make her stop so she wouldn't have to see this creature that no one should witness. He wished he could go back in time and change everything, but life did not allow that, even for visionaries like him. In his mind, he screamed, "No!" But she could not read minds.

Out of the corner of his eye, he could see her. Her face, already a knot of fear, turning to look into the room. Her mouth fell open, and the color drained from her face. She joined them frozen in time, vulnerable to whatever might happen next.

Chapter 23

The only time Cheryl was innocent of the evil in the world was the day she was born. She fought her way out of her mother's womb covered in the gunk that had supported her life up until then. Clean, soft, and swaddled, she looked up at her mother with large unfocused eyes, searching for what all children expect. It wasn't that her mother was a monster who withheld her love from her children; she had no love to give. She never had. She'd only learned pain in her own life, and that's all she had to give. Cheryl had learned not to expect anything more than pain from her mother, but that pain sent her searching for the love she saw on television someplace else. She was so hungry for love that when she thought she'd found it in Mark, she gobbled it up. She clung to it so fiercely that she didn't notice the signs that something wasn't right. When she told the story, she always said that his change came out of nowhere. He was loving one day, and the next, he was beating her. That wasn't exactly true. Looking back, she saw it all more clearly, but she was reluctant to admit it to anyone.

Mark showed her what true evil felt like. She'd hoped that when she left him, she'd be free. She'd hoped that in her absence, his evil would somehow be extinguished. That wasn't the case because, in her absence, it only grew stronger. She knew that for sure when Tanya started visiting her, but

Lady in the Lake

somewhere inside, she'd felt it all along. Now she saw it, and it was worse than anything she'd ever seen before because this was connected to her. Everything that was terrible about Mark had gotten inside of her, like a sickness that she couldn't shake. He was still here.

Cheryl gulped back her fear. Her throat tightened, and her muscles went rigid. For her, the scariest thing in the room was not the chorus of cult members dressed in white in a line around the edges of the room or the demon they had summoned. For her, the most frightening thing in the room was the ghost of her ex-husband standing directly in front of her. The flat expression on his narrow face stopped her heart.

"And here you are, right where I wanted you to be," he snarled. He took a step toward her.

Cheryl tried to step back but couldn't. Her legs were stiff. Her muscles refused to obey her commands. Fear crawled into her, pushing away any light that she might have been able to keep deep inside of her in the past.

He took another step and then another. Cheryl's breath quickened. The people along the edges of the room raised their hands and began to chant louder. The words shot out like bullets, ricocheting off the walls. She watched him with her eyes open wide. She watched every movement he made. The creature behind him stared down at her with red eyes. Its crooked nose breathed out smoke.

"How does it feel to be unable to run away? I was so confused when you left. I thought you said you would love me forever." He was so close now that if he had been a living person, she could have felt his breath on her face. Her skin tingled from his presence. He exploded in sinister laughter before jumping into her. Her body went cold as if plunged through the ice of a frozen pond. Was this what death would be for her? Was he trying to kill her just like he'd killed so many before?

**

You've never known true power until you've felt the electric surge of taking a life. You've never known how much you can control until you've teetered on the edge of chaos and not fallen over. Your determination broke me, and all this time, I was trying to break you. For a little while, I thought I had. You shuffled around the room, looking at the floor, mumbling. The fire disappeared from your eyes. I was the victor, but one day I woke up and you were gone. You tried to make me a fool. You didn't succeed. You see, you gave me a taste of what I really wanted. You showed me the blood and bruises and the cracking of bones could be more intoxicating than any drug I ever tried. You left me wanting more.

I went out looking for more. No one really satisfied me. Most people break too easily. They crumble into pieces. Most are weak, but we are different.

Do you know what to do when you discover weakness? You find a way to exploit it. Do you know what to do when you find an unlimited source of power? You find a way to take it.

That's what I'm doing, and you can't stop me.

**

Cold wind blew through Cheryl, and her body jerked. The world rushed by her. She felt like she was falling, and when she landed, she was dropped into the front seat of Mark's old truck. But this time, she wasn't the passenger. She was the driver. She looked at the large veiny hand gripping the steering wheel. Her foot pressed on the accelerator, and though she was moving in this body, she had no control. She was a passenger, watching what played out. She turned her head to look at the person in the seat beside her but only saw a blue blur of colors where the person's face should be. She recognized the avocado green shirt covered in a random splash of tiny white flowers. She remembered buying that shirt at a thrift store. A car blared its horn, and she swerved out of its path.

"Careful," the passenger said, her voice barely audible over the roar of the engine.

Anger pooled in her chest. She tightened her grip on the steering wheel and focused on the road. They approached the familiar side street, and Cheryl gave the steering wheel a yank hurling the car around the corner a little too quickly. The tires squealed.

The passenger reached out her hand, bracing herself on the dashboard.

The car bounced up the now familiar road. Cheryl immediately knew where they were going. She remembered this day now.

They passed the trees and the lake. The water's surface was still as glass. The house rose up in front of them with its sloping roof and windows set wide like eyes. When the truck stopped in front of the house, Cheryl turned to the passenger and said, "Wait here. I'll be back."

When she got out of the truck, she looked down at her legs, long and thin, encased in dirty jeans. She walked up the stairs in heavy work boots and rang the doorbell. She didn't wait long before the door swung open.

Gene stood before her, a little bit younger. He peered over her shoulder at the truck before inviting her inside. "You should've come alone."

Cheryl wiped her feet before stepping inside. "Don't

worry. She'll stay put." She walked into the living room where Patsy sat in the green velvet lounge chair.

"We've been waiting for you," she said, her expression sour. Her bright red lipstick bled into the wrinkles around her mouth.

"I'm here now." Cheryl wiped her hands on her jeans. She noticed a meekness in Mark's demeanor that she had never seen before. His speech was slow and steady, but his body language was different. He hunched in on himself, shrinking.

"Are you ready?" Gene narrowed his eyes at her. "This isn't some kind of game. You have to be serious."

Cheryl stood up taller, puffing up her chest and pulling her shoulders back. "Have I ever done anything to make you think I wasn't serious, Gene?" She tried to look confident, but Cheryl could feel Mark's heart rate increase, and his chest tighten.

"Joining the order is a commitment." Gene glanced at Patsy. "I need to be sure you have what it takes."

"That's why we do the initiation." Patty's voice was hard.

"Yeah, I know. So, where's the stuff?" Mark was trying so hard to seem like he was in charge, but now that Cheryl was inside of him, she knew how out-of-control he felt.

Patsy picked up a paper bag that sat at her feet. The opening was folded closed. She raised an eyebrow before holding it out to Mark.

He took it, and Cheryl noticed the weight of it and the way the items inside shifted. "Everything I need is in here?"

Patsy and Gene nodded. "Do what we told you, and it will be fine," Gene said.

Cheryl swallowed hard. A lump formed in her throat.

"Once you do this, the dirty work begins." Patsy grinned.

"I'm serious about this. I want to go all the way." Mark's words were more honest than Cheryl ever remembered him being.

Patsy parted her lips. "Are you certain? No one has ever done that here."

Gene chuckled. "How about you start with this first, and we'll talk about going all the way later. That could be years from now." He shook his head.

"I'm going to go all the way." Cheryl looked from Gene and Patsy. "I'm going to go all the way and further." Determination pushed into Mark. "I'll show you what true power is." Cheryl turned and left, pushing the door closed behind her. She stopped on the porch and looked into the bag. It contained a plastic bag of herbs, two candles, one red and one black, a mason jar of thick, milky liquid, and a folded piece of yellow paper. She put the bag in the back of his pickup truck before getting in and driving away.

**

What made you blind to everything that was going on? I often wondered. Were you too naive or just plain stupid? I'd been talking to demons in our backyard long before you decided to leave, but you never knew. While you could only see yourself, I was beginning to see everything and know things you couldn't even imagine with your tarot cards and your babbling on about symbolism all around us. I didn't see symbols. I saw the real thing, and it drove itself inside of me like a spike, hollowing out the parts of me that I wanted to eliminate. You thought I was a no-good drunk, and I played the part for you because, beneath it all, I was hatching a plan that would prove that I was always the most powerful one. To get true power, you have to sacrifice. You were going to be my first, but you left too soon. That's why I had to find someone else, but my search took longer than it should've.

**

It took years before Cheryl decided Mark was beyond reform. Before then, she always told herself that he would change. Sometimes he told her that he would change too, and she would believe him because she always wanted to believe him.

Now that she'd gotten the chance to slip into his skin, she knew that all the time, she was wrong. When he was being kind, he never meant it.

Mark woke from a deep dark sleep, his head pounding. He looked at his achy, bruised knuckles as he opened and closed his hand. The blinds on the far side of the room were open, letting in a flood of bright white light that made him squint.

"Cheryl!" He managed to yell despite the throbbing in his head. He found his way to his feet in the messy room. His clothes lay scattered across the floor. In only his boxers, he wandered into the living room. The curtains were drawn, filtering the sunlight through sheer yellow fabric. "Cheryl!"

He walked straight through the living room into the kitchen. Shards of glass stuck into his foot. He yelped and stepped back, falling to his butt on the living room carpet and looking at his foot. "Damn it, Cheryl!" He pulled a piece of glass the size of a quarter from his heel. Blood oozed from the wound. "Cheryl!" This time he yelled as loudly as he could, straining the muscles in his neck. Still there was no answer.

It didn't take long for him to realize she was gone for good. Somewhere deep inside, Cheryl had hoped her sudden disappearance would teach him a lesson. She hoped that in hindsight, he would've been able to see what he had done to her and never do it again to anyone else, but being alone didn't affect him like it affected her. He was angry. He smashed the rest of the glasses in the kitchen and tore the pictures off the walls, but that tantrum only lasted a few moments. What Cheryl hadn't realized before was that he was in the midst of the plan, and while her leaving was an inconvenience, it wasn't going to stop him.

Within a week, he was out cruising the streets looking for someone new. He needed someone naïve. He needed someone who would tolerate his temper and even think that his explosions were her fault. He needed someone who would stick around long enough for the spell to be complete. He thought Monica would be that someone, but he was wrong again. She was stubborn and a lot more determined than she seemed. He liked her, so he kept her around even while grooming Tanya to be his sacrifice. Tanya was easier to manipulate. Still he took his time.

He was calm on the day the ritual was to be completed. As he drove up the narrow lane, he imagined what it would feel like to finally be free of the restrictions of his own body. He wondered what it would finally be like to have control over someone else's life. Getting her into the house was easy. She drank the sedative down quickly.

He carried her inside and sat her in the lounge chair they'd positioned in the center of the room. Everyone was there. The more people who participated, the stronger the spell would be. They made a circle around her, and she sat unconscious in the chair, her eyes fluttering beneath closed lids.

Patsy walked over to Mark and handed him a red strip of fabric.

It smelled of grass. Earlier that week he had helped Patsy mix a batch of herbs that they soaked the fabric in. They had chanted and lit candles, preparing the fibers of the fabric for the ritual.

Tanya had been prepared in a similar way too. Only she hadn't known it. He had collected hairs from her brush and nail clippings and delivered them to Patsy, who would return them to him in bundles of fabric along with herbs and the tiny bones of creatures for him to hide under her bed, or in a jacket pocket, or in a backpack. He'd sprinkle magic dust on her food. He'd say incantations over her sleeping body. Preparing his sacrifice was part of his duty.

He tied the red cloth over her eyes. Patsy held her hand in the air and brought it down in a chopping motion, signaling to the others that it was time for the ritual to begin.

**

When I first learned this was possible, I didn't believe it. You know me. I don't have faith, never did. I never really believed in anything, but Gene and Patsy changed that, didn't they?

I met them at Cody's. They were both staring at me like they had a problem. It was really pissing me off because all I was trying to do was relax and have a drink before having to go home and hear you nag. I yelled across the bar, "What you looking at?"

Gene started grinning like a Cheshire cat. He walked over and sat on the empty stool next to me. Patsy stayed at their table, stirring her drink with a thin straw as she watched us. I didn't know what kind of freak thing they might want from me. You meet all sorts at Cody's.

Gene slammed the money down on the bar and told the bartender to give me another drink. "You come here a lot, don't you?"

I wasn't sure how he knew that because I never

remembered seeing them there.

"You've got something special about you." He twisted around on his stool and looked back at his wife.

I didn't know what he meant and didn't care. I tapped my fingertips on the bar and remained silent.

Gene looked back at me and shrugged. "What if I told you there is a way that you can have anything you ever wanted?"

The bartender set my drink in front of me. "I'd say you're full of crap."

He smirked. "Understandable, but what if I wasn't?"

I threw back my drink and got up. There was no way I was going to stick around for that. "I'm going," I said. When I walked out the door, I had no idea that wouldn't be the last time I saw him. They kept showing up at Cody's. They were buying me drinks, so I listened to them talk.

The first time I went to a ritual, it seemed like some crazy stuff--Gene kind of talked me into it. I agreed to it just to humor him. Before I knew it, I was chanting with a bunch of old people, calling up demons and stuff. It was crazy, but I was good at it. I guess that's what Gene and Patsy saw in me that day. They said that with me around, they could do things they'd never thought they could. They could call up power that was out of reach to them before. That's why they were after me. I didn't disappoint them.

We would sacrifice animals, but the first person we sacrificed was Tanya. It was my idea. If you want to live forever, you have to be willing to sacrifice someone else's life and, surprisingly, your own.

Gene had tried before, but he hadn't had the courage to go through with the second part. He thought I'd back out too, but I wasn't someone who backed out. You know me. I never back out.

**

Tanya took longer than anticipated to wake from her drug-induced sleep. Mark waited beside her long after the others had retired to another place in the house. She had to be conscious during the sacrifice.

When she finally came to, she leaped from the chair and ran to the front door. She fumbled with a lock for a moment before pulling the door open.

"This should be fun," he said before launching himself after her, tackling her as she went through the door. They fell out onto the porch, then stumbled down the stairs and to the grass. Tanya was able to get away. Scrambling to her feet, she began to run, screaming as she went.

He tore after her to the lake.

**

There's something about killing someone, seeing the life go out of their eyes and knowing that you did that. It's beyond anything I'd experienced before. To think I wasted all that time with you. If I just killed you from the start, I could've gotten to this point sooner.

Luckily, you came back. Look at you, giving me a second chance. That's something. It shows I affected you more than you even realized. And now, here we are. Are you ready for the inevitable?

Chapter 24

Cheryl pitched herself forward, falling to her knees. Her movements were strained and clumsy as she fought Mark for control of her body. She came this far to stop him, and that was what she was going to do no matter what.

Every part of her strained. Even as he tried to hold her back, she was dragging herself forward toward the demon in the middle of the room. Each movement she made was a battle. Mark thought he was strong, but he didn't realize how strong and stubborn she could be.

The demon didn't move from the center of the room. It stood hunched, its body rocking in time with labored breath. It reached out its long arm and pointed a gnarled finger at Cheryl. It's thick, yellow fingernails curled downwards like claws. Its black eyes looked into her.

Cheryl felt as if she was sinking away. Her vision narrowed like she saw the world through a tube. The scene around her became a circle of light in the distance. She tried to call out for help but couldn't. This was what it was like to lose complete control over her body. This must have been what the others felt when Mark possessed them.

As her body lurched toward the demon, she felt like a zombie, out of control. Mark had taken so much from her, and she had managed to get away from him to build a new life. She would not let him take the life that she had made for herself. She couldn't let him take the relationship she and Adam had built. Mark had shown her everything that he had done, the web he'd built to take her life. He didn't realize that she would never allow that.

Her mentor, Day, had taught her the words to use before. She'd learned them for a time like this, and even though she didn't have all of the things that she needed, the banishing powder in her pocket and the words were enough. Magic is a state of mind. Most times, all that matters is the intention and the strength of your will.

So with her body moving toward the demon, and Adam and Detective Haskell looking on, Cheryl did her best to call up the strength she knew she had in herself. She focused every bit of her energy on these words.

"Mark!" If she could speak, she would've been shouting. For now, her words could only exist as thoughts. "You are like the chaff the wind drives away. Therefore you shall not stand in the judgment or in the congregation of the righteous. For you make and know my way, God, but your way is ungodly. You shall be brought low and shall perish."

It was as if a rope binding her body to Mark's soul popped. Though Mark had still taken hold of her body, the grip had loosened. She could control more, slowing down the pace by dragging her left foot. She repeated the spell again as she struggled to find her coat pocket with her right hand. The words came easier now. She thought them with more force. Reaching her fingers into her pocket, she pulled out the small plastic bag Day had given her.

With each repetition, her movement became more her own. She pulled the baggie from her pocket. Her mind lagged. Her arms and legs jerked. She felt a bit like a malfunctioning robot, but still she was able to poke a finger into the side of the bag to tear a hole.

"You shall be brought low and parish." She managed to choke out the words. She flung her arm forward, and the powder flew up into the air, a cloud of dust. The dust seemed to multiply and expand as soon as it hit the air. The plume enveloped the room, making everyone cough and hack. Cheryl's eyes watered, and her lungs burned. She fell to her knees, gagging. The floor shook, and the demon in the room let out a mighty roar.

A yell exploded in her head. Mark's voice tore through her. "You can't do this!" The words echoed. She could though. She could do anything she wanted; she just hadn't realized it before.

"You are no longer welcome in this world. Leave!" Her words ripped through the air. The wind whipped around her. Everyone in the room collapsed to the floor, and the demon in the center of the room roared. He reached out a long arm toward her, but before his gnarled finger touched her, he vanished, leaving a dark stain in the spot where he stood. The wind stopped, and life rushed into Cheryl. She stood feeling more energized than she ever had. She felt like she glowed with power. The robed people along the edges of the room lay on the floor, their faces wracked with confusion.

She turned, looking at Adam, who stood behind her. Relief washed over her. "He's gone, and he's not coming back." She couldn't tell him exactly how she knew. She just did, and that was good enough for her.

**

His muscles rigid, Adam stood helplessly watching as Cheryl stumbled toward the creature in the center of the room. It was as if she were fighting against her own body, her movements jerky and unnatural. He had hoped that being a visionary would be enough to help in times like these. Unfortunately, it wasn't. All he could do was watch with his heart in his throat, and worry coursing through him. They were over. It would all be done soon. Coming to this house without more backup was a mistake. He should've forced Detective Haskell to call for backup, but he hadn't thought about it until now... until it was too late.

He couldn't move, but he could still think. His brain was more active than it had ever been, but how could thinking help? He kept his eyes on Cheryl, not wanting to let her out of his sight for even one moment.

When he was young, he went to church, a big stone building in the center of town. He didn't like the musty smell and the way the old people there pinched his cheeks. After his parents died, he and his sister kept going. He was a teenager then, and his sister had left college to stay at home and take care of him while he finished his last two years of school. Once his parents were gone, the church took on a different feeling to him. He looked forward to it. The ritual of it gave him comfort. When he sat in the pew next to his sister, he'd feel his parents there with them. He remembered reciting the Lord's prayer with the entire congregation and how the words soothed him when he felt most alone. His mind went to those words naturally now.

Our Father, who art in Heaven, hallowed be thy name;

He'd stopped believing in God when he was in college, but meeting Cheryl changed all of that. The world became a different, more mysterious place full of secrets.

Thy kingdom come; thy will be done; on earth as it is in--

Something changed. Cheryl's loping movements toward the demon slowed. She stuck her hand into her coat pocket and came out with the packet of powder Day had given her before they left. Adam had almost forgotten about it. The moments ticked by as she struggled to open it. Her feet dragging, she moved forward against her will. When she finally opened it, a cloud of dust exploded in the air, burning his eyes and clouding his vision. His nostrils stung, and he let out a giant sneeze that seemed to release him from whatever had frozen his muscles before. He pitched forward, catching himself on the doorframe. A mighty roar filled the room, shaking Adam to his core. When the dust cleared, the demon was gone, and in its place in the center of the room stood Tanya. Her bright face was no longer bruised, and her dark brown hair was dry. It hung just below her shoulders in large waves.

"He's gone," she mouthed to him. "Thank you." Her image seemed to shimmer before vanishing.

It didn't take long for Adam's focus to return to Cheryl. When he reached her side, he was eager to give her comfort, but when he reached for her, she felt electric. Energy pulsated around her. She was powerful, more powerful than he had even imagined.

"You did it." He looked around at the people lying on the floor. Then back at Detective Haskell, who stood in the doorway looking stunned.

She nodded. "He's gone, and he's not coming back."

**

They weren't there when they hauled Tanya Garrett's body out of the lake. They didn't need to be. They knew they'd sent her killer to the next life, and that was the peace Tanya had truly been looking for. Anything beyond that was for Detective Haskell to figure out. Cheryl wondered what he would tell people. To anyone who has never experienced the hidden world of ghosts and demons Adam and Cheryl lived in, none of it would seem believable.

The landscape sped by outside the car window. Cheryl reached into her purse and retrieved her phone. It had been vibrating all afternoon.

"I think we really messed up Detective Haskell," Adam said. He pulled down the sun visor.

"What do you mean?" Cheryl was only half listening. She looked at her phone screen. She had eight text messages, three from Day and five from Stephanie.

"It's obvious, isn't it?"

She tapped her finger on one of the messages to open it. Then she looked over at Adam before reading. "You're right. I was distracted. We really shook up his perception of reality, but he seemed to take it all in stride."

She had expected Detective Haskell to be in shock after what they had seen at Patsy and Gene's house, but after only a few moments of stunned silence, he jumped into action. Cheryl was genuinely impressed, but she still didn't know how he was going to write up his report.

"I'm glad that's over," Adam said.

"That's for sure." She looked down at her phone and began to read the text message from Day.

"I'm in over my head. When are you coming back?"

She scrolled down to the next one and then the next, each getting progressively more urgent. "Hurry. Before it's too late!" the final one said.

Cheryl swallowed a lump in her throat. "Remember when I said we should take our time going back home and maybe do some sightseeing."

"Yeah. You only said that a couple of hours ago."

"There's been a change in plans." She looked up from her phone. "Something's wrong. Day and Stephanie need our help."

"What's going on?" Adam asked.

"I don't know. But it sounds serious."

Adam stepped down on the accelerator, and the engine revved. They picked up speed.

Cheryl called Day. She hoped she could help over the phone, but something inside told her a phone call would be too little too late. She needed to get there in person, and she needed to get there fast.

<<<<>>>>

ABOUT THE AUTHOR

Lovelyn Bettison writes stories about things that go bump in the night. She lives in St. Petersburg, Florida with her husband, son, and dog. She loves getting letters in the mail, Thai food, and having conversations with strangers in coffee shops. Find out more about her on her website: lovelynbettison.com.

MORE BOOKS BY LOVELYN BETTISON

SUNCOAST PARANORMAL

Monster in the House
Lady in the Lake
Girl in the Woods (Coming Soon)

ISLE OF GODS SERIES

The Vision
The Escape
The Memory
The Revenge (Coming Soon)

THE HAUNTING SERIES

The Haunting of Warren Manor (Coming Soon)

More Books by Lovelyn Bettison

UNCOMMON REALITIES SERIES

Perfect Family
The Box
Flying Lessons

STARLIGHT CAFE SERIES

The Barista
The Psychic
The Widow

SUNCOAST PARANORMAL

Woman in the Window
Lady in the Lake (Coming Soon)
Girl in the Woods (Coming Soon)

ISLE OF GODS SERIES

The Vision
The Escape
The Memory
The Revenge (Coming Soon)